Destiny

Destiny

by **Vicki Grove**

G. P. Putnam's Sons • New York

Designed by Semadar Megged
Text set in 12.5-point Elegant Garamond

Library of Congress Cataloging-in-Publication Data
Grove, Vicki.
Destiny/by Vicki Grove.
p. cm.
Summary: Twelve-year-old Destiny tries to find meaning in her art in a life
complicated by three younger siblings, a mother who dreams of winning the
lottery, and her mother's unscrupulous boyfriend.
[1. Brothers and sisters—Fiction. 2. Money—Fiction. 3. Artists—Fiction.]
I. Title.
PZ7.G9275 Dg 2000
[Fic]—dc21
99-027778

ISBN 0-399-23449-7
10 9 8 7 6 5 4 3 2 1
First Impression

For my teachers

1 • IF YOU BELIEVE . . .

My mother says if you believe, your dreams will definitely come true. That's why she crosses her fingers and chants, "I believe, I believe, I truly do be-*lieve!*" before she starts scratching lottery tickets.

Miss Valentino says if you believe somebody just because they have a romantic accent and a cute lopsided smile, then you might be asking for heartache.

Mrs. Peck says to believe in myself, but that's not easy when you have to sell rotten potatoes to perfectly nice people.

The first time I was positively sure the potatoes were rotten was two weeks ago last Tuesday at Rachel's house, Jack's first stop on our weekly potato run.

It takes a little time to lug a full sack of potatoes up their seven porch stairs, especially if the potatoes are soft.

Rachel's mother, Mrs. Nichols, was standing and holding the front door open for me by the time I made it to the top. She was frowning out at the truck, giving Jack a look which I don't guess he probably saw, slumped down like he always stays while he waits.

"Destiny, that sack's too heavy for you," Rachel's mother said sharply, bending and helping me lift it through the door. *Please don't leak on Mrs. Nichols's nice hardwood floor,* I begged the soft potatoes.

I watched her cross her bright kitchen so she could get her potato bowl. She has beautiful blue glass bottles in the windows above her sink, just there for decoration.

I watched her cross back to me and the lumpy potato sack.

"Once you said you had some clothes you might give to my sisters Ethelene and Bert," I mentioned as she untied the sack and put potatoes into her shiny aluminum bowl.

She lifted one of the potatoes to her nose and smelled it. Sure enough, she wrinkled up her nose, then tilted the bowl over the opening of the sack so the potatoes she'd taken out rolled back in.

It's just a simple fact of life that potatoes go soft on you after a while. If you're lucky, they merely shrivel and grow long tangled sprouts from their many eyes. If you're not so lucky, they start to rot and smell, sometimes, like this year, as early as October. You can still carve a potato into an animal after it softens, *if* you're very careful. A potato that's merely shriveled has more uses than a soft and nearly rotten potato, artistically speaking, though it's really not that much better to eat.

"Have a glass of milk, Destiny," Rachel's mother said. "I have those clothes for your little sisters all packed up, but I was hoping I could give them directly to your mother. I've stopped by your house a couple of times, but no one answered the door."

I took the cold glass she offered, then she picked up a plate of chocolate chip cookies and held them out. They were the kind where the chocolate's runny. I put one into my jacket pocket. "Thank you," I said.

"Perhaps I could take the clothes out to your truck and have a quick chat with your stepfather," Rachel's mother suggested. "How would that be, Destiny?"

I swallowed. My hands suddenly felt so rubbery I had trouble retying the potato sack. "I just remembered that we're in an awful hurry. I was supposed to tell you that right off."

Rachel's mother nodded. She hadn't taken any potatoes, but she took five dollars from her purse and held it out to me, like usual.

"Destiny, please tell your stepfather that I'll take the clothes directly over to your house," she said.

"You could take them over and I guess if no one answers the door you could leave them there on that big tree stump in the yard," I suggested over my shoulder as I thunked that sack back down the porch stairs. I wasn't doing those leaky old potatoes one bit of good. They began leaving a snail trail along Mrs. Nichols's brick sidewalk.

When I was back inside the truck and had hauled the sack in after me, I spit on my fingers and wiped a smeary place on my window, looking for Rachel and Samantha and Crystal. I didn't see them in the yard.

"Where's them clothes I sent you after?" Jack grumbled.

It would be so awful if I told him the truth and he made me go back up to talk Mrs. Nichols into giving them to me right this minute! "She accidentally put the sack they were in out with the trash, and they got taken away to the dump," I lied.

Jack whacked the steering wheel with his hand. "Now I got nothin' but nothin' to sell at the consignment auction tomorrow night! Nothin' but six rabbits and a few old bits of scrap iron."

"You can't sell Nathan's rabbits," I said quietly, then braced myself.

I looked quickly to where Rachel's mother was still watching from the porch. Jack looked where I was looking, like I hoped he would, then worked his face into a smile.

"They're Nathan's pets," I said, knowing I was really asking for it now, witness or no witness.

Jack shoved the truck into gear. We peeled through

the driveway, leaving black smoke behind us. I bounced to my knees and looked out the back window.

Rachel and Samantha and Crystal were under the willow trees, playing something. We're all in the same sixth grade, but they didn't wave. It's always hard to know whether they don't see me, or don't recognize me through the dirty truck windows, or are just ignoring me.

2 • EVEN FLIES HAVE TO EAT

Get them stinkin' things out of my truck before you go in," Jack said when we got home. He kicked open his door and went toward the house.

I watched him step up onto the wooden box that's our front porch. The aluminum's hanging loose near the bottom of the front door from him kicking it open, so lately he's been kicking in a different place. When the door swung inward, a cheerful blast of television game show noise rushed out, almost like there were people in our living room who were crazy with happiness over seeing Jack.

I got out and drug the potato sack around to the backyard. Nathan's rabbits were in an old refrigerator back there. When we first got the rabbits Jack knocked the refrigerator's door off with a sledgehammer, then I carefully fastened some old pieces of screen wire to the front with the duct tape I asked for and got that Christmas. Now, each shelf was a separate little rabbit apartment. Two times a week, Nathan and I carefully unfastened a few inches of tape along the bottom of each shelf and cleaned the place up. Unless Nathan's legs were aching. Then I did it alone because I hated to think of the rabbits having to walk around in all that smelly mess.

I took three soggy potatoes out of the sack, twisted each one in half, and squished half a potato through each rabbit's food hole.

"Don't get your hopes up," I cautioned as they hustled up to sniff, then I turned my eyes from them and looked around the yard, planning landscaping projects.

On the ground beside the rabbit apartment complex is the old refrigerator door, and next to it is the pile of sheet metal and wood scraps Jack keeps picking up in ditches and is saving to take to the auction. Beside the scrap heap are two broken lawnmowers and a few broken television sets, and beside them the potato patch starts. It takes up the rest of the yard, except for a strip of dirt where the onions get planted every March.

I plan to put in a rose garden when the scrap metal is gone. I keep wondering if I could turn the televisions onto their backs so I could also plant flowers inside their jagged, broken screens.

Nathan came out the back door. "Hey, what you doin' to my rabbits?" he demanded.

"Feeding them potatoes," I said. "Their food's used up, remember?"

The rabbits were huddling in the corners farthest away from the potato mash, which was quickly attracting big bunches of huge black flies.

Nathan limped over and stirred up the flies by batting on the screen wire. "Shoo!" he yelled at the top of his lungs, then batted again. "Shoo you flies you!"

"Flies have to eat, too, Nate," I told him.

The rabbits had hustled forward when Nathan appeared, and they pushed their little wiggly noses against the screen wire.

I braced myself. "Nathan? We have to talk about something. I don't want to get you upset, but Jack says he's taking your rabbits to the auction tomorrow night."

Nathan jerked up straight. I could feel him sucking the oxygen out of the entire yard, getting ready to rampage.

"He might not, though," I added quickly. "It might be like the scrap iron and he won't have the energy."

"I'LL KILL HIM!" Nathan exploded into a swirling, limping whirlwind—a spitting, kicking tangle of red-faced rage you wouldn't think could fit itself into a nine-year-old's body, which is on the skinny side to boot. *"I'LL KILL HIM FIRST!"*

Nathan ran, then—just bolted, like he'd been doing a lot lately. He scrambled over our saggy little fence, then

I watched him disappear into the cedar woods that edge the railroad tracks. Was he going someplace in particular, or just escaping?

I considered following him to see, but I knew my mother would be waiting for me to come inside and help her with the girls.

•　•　•

"Hon, Roberta needs a change," my mother called as she heard me close the back door. "If I move, it'll wake Jack. Poor guy's exhausted."

When I walked into the living room, I saw that Jack was asleep on the sofa with his head in her lap.

I knelt by the playpen and stuck my fingers through the mesh, waggling them at my two little sisters. Ethelene cackled and Roberta flapped her arms and did this thing with her tongue she does—*"Thhh—thhhh—thhhh—thhh—THHHH!"* Bert's really still a baby, just eighteen months old.

"I'll tickle wickle you," I told Ethelene, then I bent over the side of the playpen and drug Bert out by sticking my arms up to the elbows under her little arms. She's usually too wet in the afternoon to give you a good grip anywhere.

I headed toward the blanket on the floor by the open box of Pampers, stiff-arming Bert in front of me so she dangled like a sack of onions.

"Go for the car!" our mother suddenly squealed behind us. "No, no, don't take the money! Stupid! Stupid! I *told* you, stupid, you shoulda gone for the car!"

"Shhh! You're gonna wake poor exhausted Jack," I warned her in a loud whisper. I thought she might tell me not to be smart-mouthed, but her eyes were glued to the TV.

My mother gets excited about game show wins. She's going to California someday soon to be on a game show and win the jackpot herself. She studies game shows all afternoon, so she's an expert. She just needs a decent win with a state lottery ticket, enough for bus fare from Gasconade, Missouri, to Hollywood, California.

A thing that worries me is that we need money, and she's always telling the winning contestants to go for the car. A car, in my opinion, would be a luxury, since my mother can keep Jack's truck running no matter what part falls off or what kind of horrible noise it starts to make.

3 • THREE SISTERS

Miss Valentino says Destiny is a romantic name and a wonderful name for an artist, which is what she is and what I want to be with my whole heart.

Mrs. Peck says in classical mythology the Destinies were these three sisters who presided over the course of everybody's mortal life.

My mother says she named me Destiny because it sounded mysterious and was the name of her very first psychic.

I wanted her to name Bert Delight, which would have gone with Destiny. Actually, before that I'd wanted her to name Ethelene Delight, then Bert could have been named Desire. Three "D" names. Sisters, in my opinion, should match.

But Jack is the father of Bert, and Roberta is Jack's mother's name.

My father's name is Randy, but my mother says he stayed the shortest and disappeared the best of any of them. I'm skinny like my mother and my hair is the same dark brown as her roots. My eyes are brown, too, though, and hers are green. So that's what I know about him—brown eyes.

I don't know who the father of Ethelene and Nathan is, but I know Ethelene was named after a woman who won nearly one million dollars on *Play for a Fortune*. Ethelene has a good luck name, which is why our mother is taking her to California with her when she goes.

Here's another good luck thing. I'm twelve, Nathan's nine, Ethelene's four, and Bert's one. When you add our ages you get twenty-six, and when you add two and six you get eight. So eight's my mother's lucky number this year, and whenever she picks lottery numbers, she always uses an eight. Last year her lucky number was four. Next year it will be three. It's always the ages of her four children added like that, and it changes every July because that's her own birthday month.

I finished taping Bert's diaper, then I went back to the playpen and lugged Ethelene out. She's almost five, and so big I can only get her out by letting her claw into my shoulders and then throwing my own self backwards so we both end up in a heap on the floor. We landed near Bert. She always thinks everyone's putting on a show for her own personal amusement, and she flapped her arms and laughed her gurgly belly laugh.

"Girls, just stop that roughhousing, I can't hear my show," our mother said without turning toward us.

"Party, Ethelene," I whispered to get her going. "Upstairs in my studio."

I was hoping she'd walk, but she crawled in fast motion over to the stairway. I grabbed up Bert and got there first, though. I sat on the bottom stair, adjusted Bert between my legs, then went up one stair at a time on my bottom, pulling Bert up after me.

"Walk up the stairs, Ethelene," I ordered. "Don't be so babyish. Walk!"

But she just sat on her bottom two stairs down from us and hauled herself up backwards like we were doing.

• • •

This house we bought four years ago with Nathan's money from when his legs got crunched by the bad lady is a two-bedroom. Jack and my mother have the big bedroom downstairs. Ethelene and Bert and I have the slope-ceilinged bedroom upstairs. Nathan has the living room sofa, and the closet in our room for his stuff.

My studio is over in the corner of our room, just past Bert's crib. It has a window—a big plus, especially when an artist is carving animals out of not-that-fresh potatoes. You can tell exactly where the studio is by the duct tape on the floor, which runs five feet out from the wall, then five feet over to the other wall. Without the duct tape, I don't know how I'd ever have enough privacy to work.

Recently I moved my air mattress and started sleeping in my studio so my mother could have the place where my air mattress used to be for her garage sale bargains. If she gets to garage sales right about closing time she can make a killing, because people hate storing away unsold garage sale stuff. Some of the killings my mother has made are a box of old *TV Guides*, a huge black garbage bag filled with pieces of foam rubber, several stacks of old-timey records you play on the kind of elegant antique record player my mother is going to buy first thing even before the ticket to California when she wins the state lottery, and six shoeboxes filled with different sizes of lids to things.

"Okay, Ethelene, WALK over to my studio for a party," I commanded when the three of us sisters reached the top of the stairs. She started crawling in fast motion toward the studio, and I couldn't nag her to walk because I was busy dragging Bert. I finally got Bert across the duct tape and planted her square bottom smack in the corner of the studio where she wouldn't wobble much. Ethelene plopped happily face-first onto my air mattress, and I dropped down cross-legged and smoothed my hands across the floor of the studio like I was smoothing out a tablecloth.

The potato-carving knife was on the ledge of the

window, by my latest batch of hippos, monkeys, and, of course, zebras. I reached over Ethelene for it, then wiped the sugary grit of dried potato off the blade with the hem of her soggy T-shirt.

I stuck my hand mysteriously into my jacket pocket. "Ready?" I whispered, looking from sister to sister, just to build the suspense. "Hocus-pocus Allidocious!"

"*THHHHHH!*" said Bert.

"Ta-dum!" I whipped out the chocolate chip cookie.

"Me—me!" Ethelene made a grab for it.

But I was too fast for her. I jerked the cookie out of her reach, then centered it on the patch of floor between us. I began carefully scoring cut lines with the knife. "One for Ethelene, one for Bert, one for Nathan, one for Destiny Louise."

I cut two of the quarters, then stopped and handed one to each of them.

Ethelene stuck hers into her mouth all at once, and Bert began squishing hers carefully with all ten fingers, bringing it up to her face to see it better. Her little eyebrows went up and down in total concentration.

"Eat that quick before your fat sister grabs it," I ordered, and Bert opened her mouth like a capital O and began cramming both the cookie and her hands into it.

I bent to cut the other half of the cookie, then changed my mind and put it back into my pocket.

4 • NATHAN THREATENS TO KILL ME, AS USUAL

Nathan slept in the yard that night, guarding the rabbits. When I rolled off my air mattress and looked out my studio window and saw him down there the next morning, he was wrapped up in this filthy old brown blanket that's usually wadded up in one of the broken television sets. At first I thought he was a big new hill the moles had made in the dirt in front of the refrigerator.

I crept downstairs and outside and put the half-cookie on the lump in the blanket that I could tell was his right shoulder. I decided I'd better not leave it there, though, or the dogs that swarm around the trash cans might get it. I tucked the cookie into the top of the blanket, where a few tufts of Nathan's wiry orange hair stuck out like delicate onion stems.

The rabbits smelled awful. I decided I'd clean their

apartments, to give them a nice last day if Jack really did take them to the auction. I straddled Nathan as I worked, and a few times the blanket squirmed, but he didn't wake up completely. Nathan's always tired in the mornings, since he can't go to bed until after Jay Leno is over and my mother and Jack get up off the sofa to go to their own room. That's why my mother lets him stay home from school a lot. She says she can't help it that she's too softhearted to wake him up.

• • •

It was after school and I was up in my studio that afternoon giving Ethelene an art lesson when Nathan came looking for me.

"You're selling my rabbits!" he hollered. "I'll KILL you!"

Ethelene looked at Nathan standing there barefoot and shaking with anger, then she picked up the scissors I was trying to teach her to use and threw them at him. "Shup!" she ordered.

"Don't say shut up," I told her. Then I turned to Nathan. "I'm not selling your rabbits, Nate," I explained. "I just cleaned their house, that's all."

"It's like when they execute you, they give you everything all nice before they do it!" he screamed, hopping all around. "They give you every food you want, even, like, T-bone steak. Or chocolate cake! And they take you out of your smelly cell and take you to this nice place to sit and visit your friends. And then they shave your head and fry you, and your eyes pop out and smoke comes out of your knees and fingers! You're killing my rabbits and I'm planning to kill YOU!"

You have to be impressed by all the stuff Nathan knows about killings and executions and things like that. He's seen every horror movie. Jack rents them. It's the thing Nathan and Jack do together, watching every horror movie.

"I didn't feed them anything, Nate. I just decided to clean their house, that's all. Did you find the cookie this morning?"

He nodded, and started sniffling.

Nathan hardly ever cries, so his tears scared Ethelene. "Shup, you idjit!" she howled.

"Don't cry, now," I whispered to Nate, pretending that I didn't notice that ropy piece of raised, white skin between his ankle and his big toe. He has four scars like that, three on his left leg and one really long one on his right. "I won't let them kill your rabbits."

Those words came out with no way I could stop them, and I regretted them the very instant they left my mouth. I knew perfectly well that Jack would take those rabbits to the auction that night, and whoever bought them would take them home and kill them and eat them. Period.

Nathan covered his eyes with his arm and ran angrily

from our room, but that didn't mean he wouldn't be expecting me to somehow protect those stupid rabbits.

My mind raced. "Ethelene, you *walk* with me to the stairs. I gotta go do something. Walk, Ethelene! I mean it! Quit being so babyish and get up onto your feet!"

I ended up grabbing around her waist and carrying her and Bert down the stairs and to their playpen with their arms and legs moving like they were crawling through the air.

I found my mother in the kitchen, leaning against the sink and looking out the window.

She had a piece of light blue paper in her hand, and she put her hand on her sharp hipbone and waved that paper through the air when she saw me.

"You ask me why I keep the doors locked and the window curtains drawn tight? You ask me why I don't answer the door or the phone? Well this is why, Destiny. This right here is why, shoved right under the front door this afternoon just like a disconnect notice!"

She dropped the paper to the floor and I picked it up and read it.

Dear Virginia,

Hope you're all well. As you know, I've sent a couple of letters asking you about your middle daughter, Ethelene. As our local Parents As Teachers coordinator, I again invite— no, urge—you to take advantage of the resources available to parents through this wonderful program. If there is any problem with a child's development, it's so much easier to evaluate and plan for at this young age. We so much want Ethelene to be prepared for Kindergarten next year, and you really should take time to call at your earliest convenience.

Yours sincerely,

Tamara Hinshaw

P.S. The program is, of course, completely free of charge.

"What exactly does 'evaluate' mean?" I asked.

My mother sank to a chair and buried both hands in her short blonde hair. You could see the purple acrylic nails she bought herself for her twenty-ninth birthday last summer shining through.

"Oh, Destiny, how should I know?" She rolled her head back and forth. "*Should* this, *should* that! I'm so tired of *should* I could just jump right out a window!"

"Well, I've got to go do something real quick. Mama? If Mrs. Nichols brings over those clothes for Bert and Ethelene, could you please just open the door and take them from her?"

She put her hands over her face. "I gotta talk to Helena," she whispered.

Helena's her new psychic.

5 • I Cuss

What I had to do real quick, of course, was run the two miles over to Rachel's house. Because I'd stupidly made that rabbit-protecting promise to Nathan, now I had to somehow get Mrs. Nichols to promise to take the clothes over to our house that very afternoon. Without those clothes for Jack to take to the auction, the rabbits were probably doomed.

When I finally made it up the steep hill Rachel and her family live on, I bent with my hands on my knees to get my breath. I could see Rachel, Samantha, and Crystal sitting in the grass and playing something under the willow trees, just like yesterday. I'd have to go almost right past them to get to the front steps, and they were already staring at me.

Rachel jumped to her feet. "It's Destiny, that *potato* girl!" she shrieked.

"She's *charg*ing!" Samantha yelled. "She's running right at us! Hide!"

Rachel walked toward me with one hand stuck up like a crossing guard. "I'm warning you, Destiny, this is private property and if you cuss at us we're calling the cops!"

I stopped, feeling like a goldfish who has fallen from his bowl and just lies there on the floor all helpless and wide-eyed and gulping. "What are you three idjits staring at?" I heard myself holler, just like Jack would have done.

Then I turned and ran back down the hill.

I was on fire as I stormed down the center of the road, burning from the inside out like this guy in one of Nathan's horror movies who died of spontaneous combustion. That potato girl, Rachel had called me. I noticed I was feeling sick to my stomach, possibly because of the cussing. Or maybe because now there was no way in the world I could keep that stupid rabbit promise.

I was running so furiously and blindly that I hardly noticed when a car pulled up beside me. "Destiny? Is that . . . you?"

It was Miss Valentino, my favorite teacher in the whole wide world, in her ultracool turquoise convertible!

"Are you on your way home, Destiny?" she asked. "Hop in. I'll give you a lift."

"Thanks," was all I could think of to say as I ran around to the passenger door.

Our school custodian, Mr. Biswalt, says Miss Valentino's car is a classic 1965 Valiant, which makes it thirty-five years old, six years older than my mother. Based on her car, he agrees with me that Miss Valentino is the coolest teacher. The other teachers drive cars from the eighties and nineties. Or one or two have a beat-up truck from the seventies, like Jack's truck is.

Miss Valentino's cool car turned out to be just as good inside. The bucket seats were white, and they squeaked and crackled when you moved.

"Destiny, are you okay?" Miss Valentino asked as we drove. "You seemed upset or something when I drove up. In fact, you still don't quite look yourself."

My ears were ringing and I could hardly hear what she was asking.

"Muh . . . Miss Valentino? Is that . . . is that part of a . . . a rabbit hanging there on your keyring?" I forced out.

"What?" She looked where I was looking, then she laughed. "Oh, my rabbit's foot! People used to put those on their keychains for good luck, Destiny. When I saw it in a flea market I thought it was a fun thing that sort of went with the car, you know? Sixties?"

I gulped. "No offense, Miss Valentino, but that was once part of an actual rabbit, and maybe even somebody's pet."

• • •

Jack actually made Nathan load up the rabbits that night. I watched it from my studio window. Jack came into the backyard with a gunnysack in one hand and the back of Nathan's neck in the other. He walked Nathan over to the refrigerator.

"You tell 'em good-bye and put 'em in here like a man," Jack ordered.

Nathan didn't talk, but his shoulders were stiffened up to ear level.

"Hear me?" Jack demanded. "This here's a two-man job. I'll do the hard part and hold open the sack. All's you gotta do is put 'em in."

Jack let go of Nathan and ripped the screen wire off the refrigerator, then he knelt to open the sack. I was pretty sure Nathan wouldn't run. He doesn't run from Jack. The rabbits didn't run, either, or try for any kind of stealthy getaway. Maybe they knew it was hopeless. Or maybe it didn't occur to them that the wire holding them was gone.

Or maybe—and this is what I truly think—they trusted Nathan. That's probably why Jack had given him the job of putting them in the sack in the first place.

Nathan just stood there with his shoulders hunched. Then he gently lifted Snowball and held her to his cheek. She nuzzled his ear, whispering her final secrets to him.

"Go on, idjit!" Jack ordered, nudging Nathan's bad leg, the one crunched the worst.

Nathan winced, then hugged Snowball, then bent and put her in the sack.

This is where I quit watching and turned and shoved my back hard against my studio wall and beat my hands on my knees.

Nathan's school class brought him those rabbits right after he got out of the hospital four years ago. He *owned* them. They were *his*.

• • •

We all five sat in the living room that evening waiting for Jack to come home from the consignment auction. We watched some reruns. We didn't talk a bit.

Nathan kept Bert propped against him and kept clutching on to her, maybe wishing she was a rabbit. Bert would normally have fussed about that, but she seemed to somehow know Nathan needed to do it and she didn't make a peep.

Ethelene sat on my lap, soaking up sadness from everybody else, so she felt like she weighed twice as much as usual. Once in a while she bounced around irritably and said, "Shup?" It was driving her crazy that no one was saying anything.

"Don't say shut up," I told her, but without much force.

Our mother put her elbow on the arm of the couch and her chin in her hand and stared at the TV screen like it was a black hole her last ounce of energy was being sucked into. I knew she felt bad for Nathan, and she was also bummed out because the phone company had disconnected our phone again and she couldn't call Helena.

"What do they expect people to do in emergencies?" she asked every once in a while. "Just hope a psychic happens to drop in right off the street?"

• • •

Jack got home halfway through Jay Leno. When we heard the truck outside, Nathan skittered out of the living room so quick that Bert, who'd been sleeping against him for the past hour or so, teetered and fell over.

I saw Nathan's shadow on the wall of the hallway. He was hiding just around the corner, listening.

"Well, them rabbits brought ten bucks each, which is something," Jack told our mother as he threw her the cigarettes he'd brought to cheer her up. Then he said, "One of those old bachelor farmers from out near Luthersburg bought 'em. Those old boys bid on most anything edible. Food ain't cheap these days, which works in our favor."

I cringed. That word "food" would slice through Nathan like a razor. Sure enough, there his shadow went, scooting down the hallway. He slammed out the back door, and our mother looked that way and frowned before she reached for her lighter.

I jumped up, crossed my arms, and glared at her. "Nathan's gone to run around alone in the dark," I told her. "You know that, don't you?" I refused to look in Jack's direction.

"That truck's idling awful rough, Virginia," Jack said.

"I'll check the timing belt in the morning," she murmured.

"He's been running off a lot lately," I said more loudly to our mother, shaking my head. "Aren't you worried?"

Jack looked at me. "Say, Destiny, I want to talk to you a minute. I had me a brainstorm while I was waiting around the auction tonight. The potatoes sold so good yesterday I think we need to add us another run. Two runs a week, starting this Friday. Maybe up the price a buck, too."

"People pay what they want to," was all I could think of to say. I could feel my chin starting to wobble as I thought, *And the potatoes are so rotten they don't take them even after they pay.*

"They most all pay the same each week. Wouldn't be hard to just take the regular pay, then stick out your hand for that extra dollar. They'll catch on all right." He stretched out in the big chair and began toeing his boots off. "Got us the usual pile of bills this week and we hardly used any taters," he bragged. "And now we got us this extra rabbit money with hardly no effort at all. Don't never let nobody say old Jack's no businessman."

I bit my bottom lip and stomped angrily into the kitchen. "I'm going to find Nathan!" I yelled over my shoulder at them, and I let the back door slam on my way out.

6 • THE PENITENTIARY

I dodged the stuff in the dark backyard and climbed over our scraggly fence, then ran full speed in the direction I was used to seeing Nathan go when he rampaged. On the other side of the cedar trees that edge the railroad tracks, I spotted him, slowed to a fast walk. His skinny-shouldered silhouette bobbed up and down against the moonlit sky as he limped along a half-block or so in front of me.

I kind of figured he might be going to Ketchum Park, since he likes to watch the middle school boys do Rollerblade stunts on the half-pipe there. But he surprised me by hanging a right at the corner of Third Street and Poplar. Something flip-flopped in my stomach. If you didn't count the abandoned shoe factory building and a big cinder-covered lot where people burned worn-out tires, the only thing out in this direction was our old trailer court, Peaceful Meadows.

Or, as Bullwhip Sally had renamed it, The Penitentiary.

I was only eight-and-a-half when we got Nathan's crunched-legs money and moved from there. Jack hadn't been with us all that long and he hadn't bought the VCR yet and started renting horror movies, so I didn't really know what a penitentiary was. You always pretended you knew things, though, so Bullwhip Sally wouldn't whip you for your ignorance.

"Walk Indian-style, you morons, or we'll all be taken by surprise and roasted alive!" she'd yell at me and the three or four other little kids who followed her around the trailer court like a bunch of puppies. We were always tripping as we tried to copy the toe-first way she said was how Indians sneaked through the forest.

Once in a while she'd whip the ground. Sometimes she'd wrap the whip snakelike around her arm from wrist to elbow. Then she'd stick her hand out, showing us how her fingers looked swollen and reddish.

"I'm cutting off my own circulation," she'd say in a low, gurgly voice. "Anybody here want that done to them?"

We'd all stand there spellbound, shaking our heads for all we were worth.

Don't get me wrong—now that I'm twelve, I know the whip Sally Purcell carried with her all the time was just some plastic toy like you'd get for a Halloween costume. But Sally was eleven and seemed as grown up to me then as I must seem to Nathan now. My guess is that she acted tough that way to get attention from us little kids because people her own age ignored her.

Anyway, like I said, I didn't really know what Bullwhip Sally meant when she called our trailer court The Penitentiary until we moved to this house and Jack brought home the VCR from Prattler's Pawn Shop and started renting horror movies. Then I learned that a penitentiary is a maximum-security prison that nearly always, at least in those horror movies, has an electric chair.

And now, as I squinted through the eye-burning, hazy air of the cinder lot and saw Peaceful Meadows glowing ahead like a flying saucer inside its high chain-link fence, I realized for the first time that our old trailer court *did* look like a maximum-security prison.

I wanted to yell out to Nathan to stop. It was a big surprise to me that my little brother would even remember this place, let alone want to come out here, especially after dark. But there he went, limping quickly through the open front gate.

Staying just far enough behind to be eaten by shadows, I followed him, still saying in my mind, *Nathan, stop!* Though I have to admit, I was thinking that pretty halfheartedly now. It had never occurred to me to come back out here, but now that I was here, I was suddenly pretty curious.

Our trailer was gone, as I knew it would be. Jack sold it right after we moved, to a woman who was going to take it to Tulsa, Oklahoma, so her daughter could use it for a beauty shop. But I was amazed to see that for some reason, most of the other trailers had disappeared, too. The only three left looked dark and deserted.

All those people and all that aluminum, just vanished into thin air. The high overhead lights every ten feet or so along the chain-link fence were just the same, though. They flickered and hummed and gave everything a bleached-out look, just like I remembered. They changed the darkness to a shadowless version of daytime, kind of like in nightmares.

A shiver started in my scalp and quickly hit my toes. I decided to come out of hiding and get Nathan out of this place, even if I had to drag him kicking and screaming. But just then, Nathan started running toward something himself.

I put on some speed and tracked him. He ran around a stand of spindly dead trees. On the other side of those trees, I glimpsed the far back corner of the chain-link fence, and there I could see the three huge Dumpsters huddled in the same place they'd been when we lived here.

There'd always been a big rain puddle in front of the Dumpsters. Everybody dumped used motor oil in that puddle, so the water was fluorescent green and had mysterious-looking swirling patterns in it. Bullwhip Sally called it Dead Man's Swamp.

I was pretty shocked to see that Dead Man's Swamp was still there, a shiny splotch of smelly water. And my little brother was kneeling right beside it, talking to some kind of hideous monster that was lounging on a partly submerged flat tire.

"Yes, my friend, dig right there for the treasure," the monster said in a squeaky-high version of Nathan's voice.

I have to admit my heart slammed hard a few times before my brain and nose told me the monster was just a very large and very dead alligator snapping turtle. I moved back behind the dead trees and watched as Nathan picked up a plastic spoon that was lying in the dirt and started digging, like he'd ordered himself to.

He didn't dig for long. After maybe fifteen minutes, his shoulders sagged and he let out a deep, tired sigh and dropped the spoon.

"Don't give up, my friend!" the monster squeaked. "Come back and dig again tomorrow, because you *know* it's got to be down there *some*place!"

•   •   •

It was late when Nathan got home, with me still sneaking along half-a-block behind. I lay wide awake on my air mattress for a long time, trying to figure out what my little brother could possibly have been digging for at The Penitentiary, of all places.

Then suddenly, I remembered Jack's new potato plan, and my questions about Nathan's life had to take a backseat to worries about my own.

7 • MISS VALENTINO FEELS HUMILIATED

Miss Valentino went to France last summer to study art.

Mrs. Peck went to Rome, Italy, a long time ago, to grieve.

My mother went to Las Vegas once, and someday she's going to California.

I wanted to go anywhere in the world to hide from Jack's new plan, but I couldn't, of course. All I could think of to do was try to find another job, and quick, so Jack couldn't make me go on that Friday potato run with those rotten potatoes.

There was a newspaper in our neighbors' trash when they put it out the next morning, but what I could read of the "Help Wanted" ads through the coffee grounds didn't sound at all promising. Cocktail waitress, electrical engineer, somebody to manage the volleyball program at the state prison in Fulton—grown-up jobs. I went to the office at school, and our secretary, Miss Buckwater, said occasionally someone wanted a middle school girl to baby-sit. But no one at the moment, she was afraid.

"I'll tell you what, Destiny, I'll put your name on the list of possibles," she told me.

I smiled back at her, but it was hard to hide my disappointment. "I need something immediately, Miss Buckwater, so I guess I better not be one of those."

I decided I'd stick around after art class last period and ask Miss Valentino if she had any suggestions for me.

•   •   •

Like I said before, even with that awful rabbit's foot, Miss Valentino is my favorite teacher ever, and not just because she teaches art.

I mean, it's true that clear back in fifth grade I was already looking forward to being able to take an elective in sixth grade, because I knew Art I had to be totally different from just having Mr. Cutcheon come to the room and show everybody some easy project, such as folding paper and snipping out snowflakes. He taught elementary art and gym, but mostly gym, by which I mean he spent most of his time during art period telling us about his days as center on his high school basketball team somewhere in Nebraska.

I'll never forget the first day of school this fall, when

I looked out the bus window and saw Miss Valentino for the first time. She was getting out of her turquoise convertible there in the middle school parking lot. No one had to tell me she was the new middle school art teacher, because Miss V. looks exactly like an artist. She wears long black skirts and this wonderful cape, and she can braid her sleek, straight hair in about a thousand different ways. She has the art room decorated with stuff she got when she lived in France last summer, which is where a whole lot of the famous artists came from.

Once back in fifth grade I asked Mr. Cutcheon if he'd like me to bring one of my potato sculptures to school sometime to show him, and he said that wouldn't be such a good idea, since food was discouraged on the bus. Which was just an excuse, because what about people's lunches?

When I asked Miss Valentino the same question, she said she'd be thrilled to see a potato sculpture at any time. So see what I mean?

I just wish the kids in Art I would shape up and cooperate with her better. I thought they'd be artists, since it's an elective. But they're mostly boys who like to draw vicious-looking comic book heroes over and over again. And there's this one girl, Jacqui, who actually *traces* unicorns and castles from picture books, then colors them with glitter markers. It's hard to believe anyone in sixth grade would think that tracing was art.

Also, Rachel, Samantha, and Crystal are in there. I

heard them talking, saying they took it because it was that or chorus or volleyball, and they hate sports and singing, both. Well, they may not hate art, but that doesn't mean they're very good at it, so they should pay better attention to all the interesting stuff Miss Valentino keeps showing us. They could also make friends with somebody who's artistic who could help them figure out how to get started on things, *if* they thought about that, which they don't.

During Art I that Thursday afternoon, Miss Valentino held up several Impressionist paintings and tried to explain to us how to use perspective. This was maybe her fifth stab at explaining that to us.

Russell half-watched with his chin on his desk, then raised his hand. Miss Valentino always looks all hopeful when someone has a question, which makes me cringe because I hate to see her keep getting disappointed.

Russell said, "You don't got to use that stuff in comics."

"And I don't get how to make it *look* like that, either," Samantha whined.

You just try! I wanted to scream, as usual. I get so frustrated in Art I, because how to do art isn't something Miss Valentino should have to keep explaining over and over again. People just have to pay attention to the lesson and then *try!*

"Yeah, in comics you don't use that stuff," Russell's friend Max said with a big yawn.

Miss Valentino bit her lips into a straight line for a

few seconds, then said, "Well, you know what? Perhaps we should go to our sketchbooks now. Let's sketch the view of the bus yard out our row of windows, using perspective so that what's closer looks bigger."

I started by drawing the grassy hill where the buses are parked. I made the bus at the bottom of the hill big, and the buses parked partway up the hill smaller and smaller as you got closer and closer to the top.

And then, I noticed that the grass on that round hill looks like my mother's short, spiky hair. So I gave the hill her face, then added a huge hand with purple nails. I made the hand look like it was curving through the sky to place the buses carefully where they belonged in the hill's hair. I put a title on the top of my page—"Bus Barrettes."

I'm trying to learn to be a close observer of life and the world in general. Miss Valentino has a sign on the door that says, "Art is a way of seeing the world," which is my new motto, too.

8 • CARPE DIEM

The bell rang and everybody stampeded out. I stayed in my chair, pretending to keep working on my sketch, which was actually done. Miss Valentino walked slowly over to the big bulletin board.

I took a deep breath for courage and went to stand a few feet behind her.

"Uh, Miss Valentino, can I ask you something? Would you know of any jobs I maybe could get?"

Miss Valentino took a thumbtack out of a Monet haystack and said, without turning around, "Destiny, don't expect a job, even a dream job you've been working toward all your life, to be what you expect."

Her voice sounded gravelly. Was she crying? A thumbtack went poinging across the room as she jerked the Eiffel Tower off the bulletin board, then let it fall from her hand to the floor.

I swallowed, not sure what to say. "Uh, see, if I'm not working, my stepfather, Jack, will make me do an extra potato run tomorrow afternoon. I'm afraid people just buy them to be nice now, all rotten like they're getting, and if we make an extra run and even *charge* more, it'll be pushing things and I just don't know what will happen."

Miss Valentino turned toward me then. She took a soggy-looking tissue from the pocket of her long black skirt and pressed it against her eyes. She was as pale as a suffering princess in a sad book, and the tip of her nose was red.

"You'll feel humiliated, that's what will happen. You give up everything to come home from France—the Eiffel Tower, all those romantic cafes where you drank that great French coffee with Marceau, who was the cutest guy and said the most wonderful things, though of course if you believe someone just because they have a romantic accent and a cute lopsided smile, you might be *asking* for heartache. And of course there was the Louvre, which is *the* greatest art museum in the entire world. You give up romance, culture, just *everything,* because all your life you've wanted to teach and this job opens up in your very own hometown. Then you try to get across the excitement that art is, and you think people will be all enthusiastic and eager, but then your students just . . . just . . ."

She pressed her fingertips against her forehead and her eyes got wide. "Oh, Destiny, I don't know what came over me! I'm really sorry." She closed her eyes and shivered. "I know you won't believe this, but even at age twenty-four you don't have everything all figured out."

She was right—it was nearly impossible for me to believe you could get to twenty-four and not have life all figured out, especially when you were so pretty and had actually sold three watercolor landscapes and could double-braid your hair like hers was today. It was too depressing to think about.

Miss Valentino leaned back against her desk and mopped her face with her sweater cuffs, then she straightened her shoulders and gave me a limp smile. "Sorry to be such a goof, Destiny. Uh, at the gym I go to they hire kids to clean up the sinks and empty the wastebaskets and things like that. Oh, no, wait—I think you have to be sixteen. I'll ask, but I'm pretty sure that's their policy. Maybe state law."

I nodded. Why had I told her that embarrassing stuff about people just buying the potatoes to be nice? I hadn't told *anyone* about that. In fact, I hadn't even let myself *think* that in so many words.

I spotted the Eiffel Tower's thumbtack glittering on the floor under the little paint-mixing sink, picked it up, and put it on the edge of Miss Valentino's desk. We both looked at it for a second, then I cleared my throat and said, "You don't need to ask about jobs at the gym. Thanks for thinking about it, though."

I started toward the door.

"Destiny, wait! I just remembered something! You're a good reader, aren't you?"

I turned back toward her. To some people reading is a school subject, but to me it's always seemed more like just breathing or something. "I read all the time to my little sisters," I said with a shrug. "And to Nathan, when he doesn't run away."

Miss Valentino crossed her arms and her eyes lit up.

"In the teacher's lounge they were talking about Mrs. Peck, the woman who used to teach Latin at this school when I was in seventh and eighth grade myself. Ten years ago—whew! They were saying she's lost most of her eyesight now, and she's looking for someone to read to her occasionally. Now, I don't know what she's willing to pay, or even *if* she's willing to pay. And maybe she's looking for an adult, for companionship. But I know where she lives, and my Valiant is in the parking lot, and I'm sick to death of moping around. Shall we check it out?"

I eagerly nodded my head.

"Great! Let's do it, then! *Carpe diem!*" Miss Valentino threw her wonderful green cape around her shoulders, hitched her huge brown backpack over it, then switched out the lights and breezed out the door.

Before I ran to catch up, I quickly grabbed the Eiffel Tower picture off the floor and shoved it into the back of my social studies book. Mr. Biswalt would have swept it into his big trash container and smashed it down with his boot.

• • •

I carefully avoided looking at the dashboard of Miss Valentino's cool car, where that white fur foot would be dangling from her keyring. Instead, I looked over my shoulder at the backseat, which was taken up by a huge box filled with good stuff for art—colored paper and crepe paper rolls and pieces of wire and wooden dowels, stuff like that.

"I have *you* to thank for those supplies, Destiny," she said when she saw me looking back there. "I took the advice you gave me last month and checked out the consignment auction. A lady that used to have a craft store brought that box, and I got it for just eleven dollars! What a bargain, huh?"

I definitely didn't want to think about the consignment auction, so I said, really quickly, "Miss Valentino, what was that you said back at the school, that carpy thing?"

"*Carpe diem.* It's a Latin phrase, and it means 'seize the day.'" She looked at me and smiled, then punched the air. "Seize the day!"

"'Seize the day!'" I echoed, thinking, *Someday I want to be exactly like you, Miss V.*

9 • MRS. PECK, THE TEACHER

Pretty soon Miss Valentino pulled to the side of the road, and I looked around and noticed we weren't really in town any longer, though we weren't exactly out in the country, either. There were thick lines of trees on each side of the road, and a few mailboxes stuck out of them like stubby toes poking out of too-short green blankets. The mailbox closest to us read "Ernest W. Peck."

"We turn here to get to Mrs. Peck's house," Miss Valentino whispered to me. "Her lane is nearly impossible to see from the road because it's surrounded by all those cedar trees."

"So, she's got a husband?" I whispered back, nodding toward the mailbox name.

She shook her head. "He died a long time ago, even before I was her student."

"Is she . . . nice?" I whispered. For some reason, I doubted that we'd be whispering like this if she was really nice.

Miss Valentino took a deep breath and held it, thinking. Finally she said, "Destiny, when I took Latin from Mrs. Peck in eighth grade, she gave us the assignment of putting on a little play about Julius Caesar. She told us our midterm test would be this play—if we followed through with it, we'd get an A, if we didn't, we'd fail. There were only seven in our class—Latin was an elective and what kids called an 'egghead' class. Anyway, the seven of us practiced hard, and learned our lines in Latin, and our mothers made us togas and everything. But that semester the school soccer team was really fantastic, and the school board decided to dismiss school the day of the state tournament so that everyone could go cheer for them. The trouble was, that also happened to be the very day we Latin class people were supposed to perform *Caesar and His Times* for a few book club ladies Mrs. Peck had gathered up to be our audience."

I shrugged. "So she changed the date of your performance, right?"

Miss Valentino chewed her lip. "We went to her and asked her to, but she said no. It was set, she said. She wouldn't discuss it further, she said. You had to know her—her feathery white hair, those piercing blue eyes. She looked a lot like I'd always imagined her idol, Julius Caesar, looking. We were shocked by her attitude, but no one dared to argue. The principal was on our side because of school spirit and everything, but even he wouldn't argue with Mrs. Peck. Like I said, you had to know her."

I was *about* to know her, though. I gulped. "So, you skipped the game?"

"Three kids skipped the game, four kids skipped the performance. She flunked the four who skipped the performance, gave them an F for a midterm test grade."

Miss Valentino had been squinting at the trees. "Okay, now I see the entrance," she murmured as she put the car in gear. "I'm not sure 'nice' is the word I'd use for Mrs. Peck, Destiny. But I admire her a lot or we wouldn't be here."

"She gave you an A, then."

"No, actually I flunked."

Miss Valentino nosed the little Valiant into a narrow lane that split the trees. All the way up that steep lane, tree branches reached up from both sides to meet in the middle, like dancers clasping hands to make an arch. We were traveling through a tunnel of beautiful leaves, and the sunlight that got down to us was spangled and broken into pieces.

When we finally came out at the top of the hill, we blinked from the brightness. I could see Mrs. Peck's house ahead. It was square and gray, made out of glistening stone. There were two big white pillars in front, and there were lots of flowers all around. Some of them were roses. There were even some statues standing around here and there in those flowers. Not statues of little dwarves or flocks of chickens like I'd seen in yards in town, but real statues like in art books. The best one was a blindfolded girl with two birdbaths hanging from her hand.

I didn't say so out loud, but it was the house of my dreams, so stone solid you could tell nothing it held would be worn through or even cracked. You couldn't imagine things inside a house like that smelling spoiled or ending up tangled in a mess all over the floor.

Miss Valentino drove more slowly, with her elbows up, tense and pointy.

"Are you changing your mind about talking to her about me?" I whispered.

"It's just that she's a . . . a *tea*cher," Miss Valentino whispered back.

"*You're* a teacher," I pointed out, but I thought I knew what she meant. There are teachers, and there are *tea*chers.

We reached the pillars and just idled there in front of them, both of us leaning toward my window and staring wide-eyed at the queenly white porch of the house.

Then suddenly, a sharp voice came from right behind our backs, so close we both about jumped out of our skins.

"If you're those cable *tele*vision people, I thought I made crystal clear to you on the phone that I'm not the *slight*est bit interested."

Mrs. Peck was standing behind a giant rose bush not ten feet from us.

"Mrs. Peck!" Miss Valentino exclaimed, jumping from the car. I got quietly and quickly from my own side, but kept the open door in front of me like a shield.

She was exactly like Miss Valentino had described her—white, and piercing. In fact, her hair was as white as Snowball's rabbit fur had been, and her eyes looked like electrified pieces of the sky. She was holding a hoe in one hand, but you wouldn't have for one second thought she was a real farmer. She was definitely a *tea*cher, retired or not.

Mrs. Peck just looked at Miss Valentino, squinting like she was thinking hard.

"Miranda Valentino," she finally said, pronouncing each syllable separately and slowly. She still wasn't exactly smiling, but now there was a tiny dent of a curl at each edge of her straight, thin mouth. "And, Miranda, is this one of your students?"

"You knew I was teaching?" Miss Valentino suddenly sounded like a girl, not a grown-up. "Oh, golly, Mrs. Peck, I just can't believe you knew that! Or that you even remember me!"

Mrs. Peck raised her chin and smiled a little more obviously. "I remember most of my students, and take a continued interest in their lives. I confess a particular interest when one of you decides to become an educator. Now, Miranda, if you please, introduce your protégée."

It took Miss Valentino and me both a couple of seconds to realize I was the thing she was talking about, the protégée.

"I'm Destiny Louise Capperson," I said, hustling around to stand by Miss Valentino. "I'm in sixth grade at the middle school, and Miss Valentino is my art teacher." I was so nervous I could barely breathe, and somehow because of that I added, "I just love art. All art."

Mrs. Peck did that squint again, only this time she squinted right at me. *All art*—stupid!

After about a million years, she looked at Miss V. again. I felt like a gigantic white bird had had me in its clutches and had finally let me drop back to the ground.

"I'd like to offer you two ladies some refreshment, but as you see I was just digging out my dahlia bulbs," Mrs. Peck said. "I could arrange at least some tea, under the portico perhaps?"

"No, Mrs. Peck, thank you, but we really can't stay," Miss Valentino said. I saw two patches of bright pink on her neck, one on each side. "We came out to, well, ask you about a . . . a rumor at school that you're perhaps, well, looking for someone to read to you. I mean, someone, some people, were saying that your vision is, well, deteriorating. And that you're possibly in need of . . ."

Mrs. Peck tapped her hoe handle on the ground, hard. I braced myself, halfway expecting the dirt to split and smoke to come billowing out.

"I detest rumor," Mrs. Peck said sharply. "Especially rumor of my own deterioration."

"That's certainly understandable," Miss Valentino said quickly, gulping. She groped behind her for the handle to her door. "Well, I do appreciate your remembering me, Mrs. Peck, and I'm sorry we've interrupted your . . ."

Meanwhile, I was hurrying around to my own side of the car, trying to be invisible.

"You there!"

I froze.

"You there, Destiny Louise Capperson, the art lover. What have *you* to say?"

What did *I* have to say? I could only think of one thing. It didn't make a lot of sense, but it was the freshest thing in my brain, I guess. "Thanks anyway, Mrs. Peck. And *carpe diem,* okay?"

Mrs. Peck's eyes flashed. "Assuming she's an excellent reader, your protégée is hired, Miss Valentino. She'll start, if she's able to, tomorrow afternoon."

•   •   •

We bounced happily in our seats all the way down the lane, then when we got far enough along the asphalt road so that Mrs. Peck couldn't possibly see us from up on her hill, Miss Valentino pulled the car over so we could high-five each other. A lady across the road who was watering her bushes and watching us caught the spirit and whirled her hose around in the air, laughing.

"That was such a cool move, talking to her in Latin like that!" Miss Valentino raved, as though I'd done it on purpose.

That made my stomach tighten.

"Okay, you need your mother to send a note to school tomorrow saying you're supposed to ride bus four home instead of your usual bus seven," Miss V. started eagerly explaining. "I'll tell them in the office about your job, and bus four will let you off right at Mrs. Peck's lane. Then when you get finished, you can catch a town bus home at the corner past her mailbox. Metro Bus eleven goes to your neighborhood." She reached in her backpack and rummaged out two quarters. "Your first day's fare—a good luck gift."

"Thanks, Miss Valentino," I said, taking the quarters. I flashed her another huge smile, but I wished she wasn't quite so excited about this, because really—what if Mrs. Peck thought I talked Latin like that all the time? What if she couldn't stand me in English?

10 • PROMISES, PROMISES

When Miss Valentino let me off at my house, there were two boxes balanced on the stump by the porch. I couldn't carry them both at once, but I picked up the top one. "It's just me, so open up!" I yelled, and a few minutes later my mother opened the front door a crack, checking to be sure the person yelling with my voice was actually me.

"If you'd quit taping that garbage sack over the living room window, you could see who's outside a lot quicker," I grumbled. I shoved backwards through the door and plonked the box onto the floor. "Rachel's mother must have left these. They're the baby clothes she said she'd give us. I'm going back out for the other box, and these are too heavy for me to have to wait a million years, so *don't lock me out!*"

My mother shut the door behind me, but opened it a crack again when I got close.

"For your information," she told me, "the garbage sack keeps the glare off the TV, and gives us privacy." She went back over to the couch and sat down again beside an old newspaper covered with greasy black truck parts.

I dropped the second box beside the first one and began ripping into the tape that sealed it. "Rachel's mother wants to talk to you about something," I said.

My mother was blowing as hard as she could into one of those greasy parts, a little whistle-shaped thing. "Fuel filter's clogged, for one thing," she murmured, trying to peer through it. She turned to me. "She knocked on the door when she left these boxes this afternoon and about scared me half to death. I was having the best little nap, and when she finally quit her hammering, I couldn't get back to sleep."

"What if she came over here to tell you there'd been an atom bomb dropped, and you had half an hour to get your children to shelter or they'd all die of radiation poisoning?"

My mother was craning her neck to see into the box I was opening. There was a little black grease circle on her mouth. "You s'pose she tucked any money in there anywhere?" she asked.

"Or what if she came over to tell you there's a tornado headed right toward our house and we have fifteen seconds to get to shelter?"

"I'da heard that on the TV," she answered. She sat down cross-legged on the floor and pulled the second box over close to herself. "I need a few bucks for cigs, and Jack's gone with a couple of friends and all the money in the house to get our lottery tickets." She began slicing at the tape with her long acrylic thumbnail.

Why was Jack getting lottery tickets on Thursday? He usually got the tickets on Tuesdays, after the potato run. He only got them a different day if he could find somebody to give him cash for some of our food stamps. Then it hit me.

"He's using the money from Nathan's rabbits." I wanted to make that accusation sound sharp and slow and solemn, like Mrs. Peck talked. But I think it came out pretty squeaky and fast, like *I* talk.

"Oh, Dess, don't start, okay?" my mother said, turning her box over and letting everything come unfolded and pile out into her lap and onto the floor all around her.

"Where *is* Nathan, anyway?" I asked. That made me think of my sisters, too, and I looked over at the playpen. They were sprawled together asleep, Ethelene's head on Bert's left leg.

"He's upstairs," she answered. "He's grounded up there for running away last night and coming home so late. And Destiny, I'm mad at you about that, too."

"By the way, I got a job," I told her, grabbing a double armload of the clothes. "I start tomorrow right after school, so you have to tell Jack I'll give him whatever part of my pay he wants, but there is no way I'll be able to make an extra potato run with him."

I hurried upstairs before she could say anything back. I shoved the clothes into Bert and Ethelene's drawers, then I took a deep breath and knocked on the closet door.

"Go away!" Nathan called out. "I'm about to KILL you!"

"You better watch what you yell from in there," I told him through the keyhole. "You think it'll always be me knocking, but someday it just might be Jack."

I opened the closet door. Nathan's pile of clothes and stuff comes up to about my waist. Nathan was lying on his back on top of the pile, braced on his elbows so he could kick at me with both cowboy boots. He caught my right jaw before I could get ahold of his ankle. It really hurt, so much that tears came to my eyes.

"Now, Nathan, you just stop, and I *mean* it!"

He scrambled to sit up. He's not used to actually connecting when he tries to kill me.

"Don't tell," he said quickly, looking scared.

"I just might if you don't quit." I flopped back against his stuff, rubbing my hurt jaw.

After a minute, I turned around and looked closely at him. His chin puckered up and wobbled. "You *promised*," he said, sending so much anger in my direction that it burned.

"I know," I whispered. "I'm sorry, Nathan. I just couldn't protect your rabbits."

He started to slide past me, and I knew he was going to rampage, so I quickly blocked the closet doorway with both arms. "Nathan, I've got to tell you something! I followed you last night. I know you went out to our old trailer court, and I'm not going to tell on you and I'm not even going to ask why you're digging out there. BUT, you have to make a deal with me that you won't go out there alone from now on. It's too creepy. If you quit going alone at night, I'll go with you in the daytime and help, okay?"

To my surprise, he didn't angrily accuse me of spying or anything. "Tomorrow?" he asked eagerly.

"My new job starts tomorrow. But we'll go Saturday, okay?"

Before I knew what was happening, he just sort of lurched forward and suddenly he was hugging me tight with his legs around my waist and his arms around my neck.

"You promise, Destiny?" he asked, as though I hadn't just spoiled my reputation as a keeper of promises with the rabbit thing. It breaks my heart when he keeps trusting me and trusting me like that.

"Okay, promise," I whispered into his sweaty hair.

11 • CRYSTAL CHOKES ON A DREAM DATE BARBIE HEAD AND MRS. PECK ANSWERS A HARD READING QUESTION

C rystal nearly choked to death on a Dream Date Barbie head at afternoon recess the next day. I noticed her there by the bikestands holding her neck and retching, so I ran over to her. There was a little strand of shiny Barbie hair hanging from the corner of her mouth, so I yanked on it and the Barbie head popped right out and hit the ground.

Nobody plays with Barbies in sixth grade, of course, but Samantha and Rachel and Crystal sometimes bring decorated shoeboxes full of Barbie arms and legs and heads, then make a game of running around the school-yard throwing those parts at each other.

I don't know why Crystal put a head in her mouth. After I yanked it out of her mouth, she picked it up by a small strand of its hair and said, "Thanks for saving my life, Destiny. Want to throw once?"

I looked at the spitty head and said, "No, but thanks for asking."

Babyish game or not, I thought it was amazing that after nearly calling the police on me a mere three afternoons ago they'd actually ask me to join them for a throw.

• • •

All that afternoon I thought about my new job and tried to get over being so nervous about it. Miss Valentino made a point of giving me a thumbs-up sign when she passed me in the hall, which made me feel good, but in another way made me even more nervous.

On bus 4 I tried to go over in my mind some things I could say to Mrs. Peck, but I kept getting interrupted by people telling me I was on the wrong bus and asking what was wrong with my jaw, which was pretty bruised where Nathan had kicked me.

I had a chance to practice a few phrases out loud as I walked up Mrs. Peck's beautiful, tree-sheltered lane. "I am just so very pleased to be under your employ," I thought I might open with. I'd read that sentence once in a book. "Your wish is my command, Mrs. Peck." Did that sound too much like something a genie would say? "Mrs. Peck, I've arrived to do your bidding." That was another book sentence, but I wished I could remember what kind of book it was from. Was reading bidding, or was bidding mostly going out to have a sword fight for someone or something like that?

When I got most of the way up the lane, I stopped and closed my eyes and listened to the magical sound of all those overhead leaves brushing together, reaching up and grabbing sunlight and playing with it like they were slender green hands. I could have stayed there in that lane forever and been completely happy. I held out my arms and twirled, and even with my eyes closed I could feel the flickering sunlight drip through those playing hands to paint me with dancing light.

"My, I must say your punctuality is impressive, Miss Capperson."

I stopped. Mrs. Peck was standing at the very top of the lane. She was framed by the trees, holding her hoe in the same way she'd held it yesterday.

She had a little black machine hanging on a long cord around her neck, and while I stood there gulping and trying to remember at least one of the possible things I'd been going to say, she pushed a button on it and held it to her ear. It was a sort of talking clock. *"It is now three-forty-seven. Beep!"* came a strange little robotic voice. *"It is now three-forty-eight. Beep!"*

"Now, Miss Capperson, I would like to clarify something if I may," Mrs. Peck said. A breeze came up and her short white hair fluttered like a crown of silver leaves. She was staring at the lower part of my face. Was she wondering about the swollen jaw Nathan had given me? "The rumor your teacher heard about the deterioration of my vision was like most rumors—based on a grain of truth, but lacking the sort of precision that makes the information useful. I have a condition called macular degeneration. In spite of several laser surgeries, it has progressively destroyed my central vision, though I continue to have some fair degree of peripheral vision, especially in my left eye. I can garden, can't drive. Am able to mend the fingers of my gardening gloves, but can't thread a needle. Can find the phone and answer it with no trouble, but can't dial it quickly enough so that the crazy thing doesn't time itself out and beep in my ear halfway through. And so on and so forth."

I swallowed. She was still staring at my jaw. "My brother accidentally kicked me in the face last night," I explained. My heart was really pounding.

She jerked slightly like that had taken her by surprise, then she came down to me and took hold of my wrist. She bent and looked closely at my shoulder. "My, my, I see it now. Nasty. Come follow me and we'll see what we can find in the flower beds to put on it."

It turns out that because of this macular degeneration, a person looks at your chin when she wants to see your eyes. She looks at your shoulder to see your jaw. It's like when you focus on the TV in front of you and spy out the left corner of your eye on your sneaky sister crawling toward the popcorn bowl.

Mrs. Peck led the way up the path to her wonderful garden, and I felt a little less nervous when I noticed that from behind she looked more like a normal tall lady and less like Julius Caesar. Her skirt hitched up a little with each step, showing skinny white legs with thick blue veins. Each time her left foot came down she leaned hard on her hoe, and her knuckles were round and knotty and covered with brown spots.

Can garden, can't drive. Can mend, can't thread. Can answer phone, can't dial it.

"Uh, Mrs. Peck?" I ran timidly from behind her. "What about reading? I mean, can you do *it* now?"

She stopped walking and straightened her shoulders, wrapping both hands around the hoe handle like she was thinking of using it for a weapon. She didn't turn to face me. Her silence was awful, like Nathan's silence right before he starts to rampage.

Even the trees that guarded the lane behind us suddenly quit fiddling with the sunshine and got quiet. Sure enough, like Nathan could, Mrs. Peck was sucking up the oxygen.

Then, just as I'd decided I'd better apologize because I was sure she was sort of mad at me, like she'd been sort of mad at Miss Valentino for mentioning those rumors of her deterioration, Mrs. Peck finally answered.

"No, alas, that greatest of all pleasures is now denied me by some avenging Fury."

12 • MY MOTHER WAITS FOR A REPAIRMAN TO ARRIVE

N ow take that nasty gook off your face this instant, Destiny Louise," my mother said when I got home. "I mean it, I won't have you walking around here looking like some pervert."

"It's aloe mash, and it feels just wonderful," I told her. "Mrs. Peck made it for my jaw before I read to her this afternoon. It's practically all unswollen already."

"Oh, okay then, I thought it was some weird new art you were doing on yourself." She reached for the remote, which was on the floor, half-buried under the baby clothes that were still down there from yesterday. Ethelene was sleeping on a pile of them she'd pulled together into a pillow for herself.

"While she was sorting out the books she wants me to read to her, Mrs. Peck told me all kinds of neat stuff about the Romans, too."

"That's nice, hon. Rome must be a real nice country with all those beaches and all. Listen, would you run into the kitchen and start the spaghetti meat? I've got to stay in here and listen for the door. Jack's friend Earl is coming over. He knows how to tap into cable for free, and he's going to hook us up this afternoon."

I'd been thinking about telling her some of the Roman stuff, but I changed my mind.

●　　●　　●

When I went into the kitchen, I saw that the table was covered with truck parts. I left them in the same order my mother had put them in, but moved them closer to the center of the table to give us room to eat dinner.

I was stirring a can of spaghetti sauce into the browned ground beef when I heard a knock on the door. "Well, it's about time, Earl," I heard my mother grumble as she clicked off the TV. The TV going off almost always wakes Ethelene up, and I heard her whine, "Shup, you!" in a grouchy, half-asleep way. Then I heard my mother yank open the front door. Then things were totally quiet. The crackle of the spaghetti meat was all you could hear for a few seconds, and I got that tingly feeling along the back of my neck you get when you can tell something's wrong.

Finally I heard a familiar voice come from out on the porch. Rachel's mother.

"I'm Nancy Nichols, Mrs. Capperson. Surely you

remember me from the social services office downtown? I just thought I'd drop by to be sure you got the clothes I left all right."

I bit my lip, wishing the clothes weren't strung all over the floor.

"Yes, I got them, and I thank you," my mother said.

"And if you don't mind, there's something I was hoping you'd have just a minute to talk about." I could tell from her voice that Rachel's mother was still out on the porch, probably wishing my mother would let her come in.

"Well, to tell the truth, my children are needing their dinner," my mother said. "And I'm expecting a . . . repairman."

"I'll just take a second, Mrs. Capperson. May I call you Virginia? Listen, when I introduced myself to you in the office, I told you I was teaching the adult education classes for our county. I told you then that I would love to have you in our high school equivalency program as soon as possible. I'm certain you've gotten the letters our office has recently sent, explaining that cutbacks will soon make most state aid contingent on full-time employment. You'd be so much better prepared to find a good job if you had your high school diploma, Virginia."

There was another long silence then, broken only by Ethelene half whining, half humming. Then Bert woke up upstairs in her crib and began screaming her head off.

"Well as you can hear I've just got to be going now," my mother said in a relieved-sounding rush. "Anyhow I'll be getting a big bunch of money very soon, so we won't be needing that state check or even food stamps for very much longer. Night, now."

The door whooshed closed and I heard my mother thunk her back against it.

•   •   •

She came into the kitchen a few minutes later, carrying Bert. She slid Bert into her high chair and I went over and blew on Bert's toes to see her gurgle and grin. My mother looked at the truck parts and sighed, then walked quietly over to the sink and looked out the window. "I'll file down the spark plugs to see if that helps, but I'm very afraid that carburetor might need rebuilding," she said sadly. Then she said, "Dess? When we were speaking earlier, when I referred to Rome as a country? Well, I remembered that it's most certainly not, it's a city in the country of Italy. I just wanted you to know that I did know that and your mother isn't stupid or anything, okay?"

I shrugged. "Okay," I said. "The spaghetti meat's about done. Do you want me to start the water for the noodles?"

She got down the big noodle pot herself and turned on the water. "Just because I didn't graduate from high school, I'm not stupid. Life knowledge is what counts, right? I quit to have *you,* after all. Or at least, I was planning to go back, until I got pregnant."

"I know," I said. I leaned down with my elbows on the table and watched Bert chase a leftover soggy Cheerio around her tray. "Mama, you know how you have a dream sometimes, and in the dream the sunlight is all flickery, and the wind brings all these flower smells to you, and you get a totally happy, peaceful feeling? That's how the lane is up to Mrs. Peck's house."

"Huh," she said. "When your daddy and I got married in Las Vegas, I smelled a kind of incense in one of those boutiques they've got out there that hit me that same way."

"Also, Mama, when you told Mrs. Nichols you were getting a big check soon, were you talking about the quiz show win out in California?"

She sighed. "I s'pose. Or something. I don't want to think about it now, Dess, okay?"

"Want me to tell you some stuff about the Romans?"

"Not especially, hon. Not right now, okay?"

• • •

Late that night I heard my mother talking on the phone.

"Helena, I've just got to have some luck!" I heard her say. She sounded really desperate, like she might be crying and everything. "I'm losing my mind! Who knows where Jack is half the time here lately, and everybody's on my case about money and half-a-dozen other things. Tell me what you see in the cards for me, girl, and make it something good, big, and *soon,* all right?"

I folded my arms across the top of my head so my ears were covered tight. I imagined myself walking up that leafy lane to Mrs. Peck's house. I had one of my little sisters by each hand. They were wearing clean white dresses, and Nathan was skipping along high in front of us like he used to do when his legs were still perfect.

I must have fallen asleep then, because suddenly it was later and my mother was shaking my shoulder.

"Destiny! I just have to tell someone before I pop!" she whispered in this happy, excited way. I slitted my eyes barely open. "We're right on the very verge of hitting the jackpot, Dess! Helena did a complete psychic reading on me, and she says it'll be real, real soon now, and all we have to do is hang on tight and believe! I could just scream with happiness and relief. Destiny, can you hear me? Destiny!"

I don't know just why, but I kept on pretending not to be awake.

13 • DIGGING

When I went with Nathan to dig the next afternoon, The Penitentiary seemed less scary than it had at night, but in a way, even more strange. Now you could see big sticky-brown rectangular patches where the grass had been killed beneath each of those missing trailers, and each of the abandoned lots still had its white electrical hook-up pole at the top edge, standing there like a tombstone.

I hate to sound gross, but the place really did look more than anything like a gigantic cemetery where forty-foot-long giants had been buried and the grass hadn't grown back yet over their graves.

"Do you remember much from when we lived here?" I asked Nathan, trying not to feel depressed as we walked toward the motor oil puddle. I'd noticed the curved black pole where Mr. Landers had hung his parakeet cage in the summer lying on its side in the dirt.

"No," Nathan answered.

I pointed. "Our trailer was right over there, in that lot right next to the lot with that big metal tower still on it. That tower belonged to our neighbors, the Watleys. They had a TV antenna attached to it. Everybody else just used rabbit ears on their TV's."

Nathan stopped and glared at me.

"Not *real* rabbit ears, Nate. That's what you call those two pieces of metal that sit on top of a TV to give you better reception."

Still looking a little suspicious, Nathan started walking again. "I remember you taking me to Dead Man's Swamp and telling me it was where pirates buried treasure," he said. "And I remember Ethelene screaming her head off all the time."

"She was just a tiny baby," I explained. "They all do that."

Pirate treasure? And then I remembered. One day not too long before his legs got crunched in the car wreck, I took Nathan walking. He was too little at four-and-a-half to run with us big kids, but I took him walking around the court sometimes. That day somebody had left a smashed-up plastic boat in the dirt near the puddle, so I told him a story about how Dead Man's Swamp was filled with wrecked pirate ships and about how the pirates used the beaches around it to bury their treasure for safekeeping. It was better than telling him the story Bullwhip Sally had told us, about the water being greenish like that because it was filled with the rotting fingers of bank robbers, fingers that the police routinely cut off in jail as part of the robbers' punishment.

We rounded the clump of dead trees, and the smell of the alligator turtle hit me. I stopped, clutching my stomach with one hand and crimping my nose with the other. Nathan ran on ahead and dropped to his knees by the plastic spoon.

"I've been digging and digging, but I haven't found the treasure yet!" he called to me.

I grabbed air through my mouth and called back, "Nathan, come on, you *know* that treasure stuff was just a story. I was always telling you stories when you were little!"

"Sure I know that, Destiny," he said, rolling his eyes at me. Then he looked over at the sagging carcass of the alligator turtle. Then he looked back at me. "That pirate treasure is *not* the treasure I'm talking about. *He* says the *real* treasure is still out here in the spot where I buried it, and he says you're supposed to let go of your nose so you can talk normal and come help me dig for it right this minute."

I reluctantly went over and dropped to my knees beside Nathan. There was a long line of shallow holes he'd already dug in the hard dirt. I'd brought my own personal scissors from my studio to dig with, and we took turns using them. You could dig about six times as well with them as you could with that stupid plastic spoon.

"So, when did you bury treasure out here?" I asked Nathan casually when we'd been digging for a while. I felt hot and messy, and my fingers ached from digging in the hard-packed dirt. This was aggravatingly stupid, but I couldn't let Nathan think that I didn't believe he'd buried treasure or he'd *never* give up. It was better just to play along.

"The same day that I got it," he answered.

"And when was it, exactly, that you got this amazing treasure?"

"The morning before my legs got crunched," he answered absentmindedly, making a little grunt as he shoved the scissors under a rock that wouldn't move.

My ears rang. "You . . . got treasure the day of the accident?"

"Yeah, from Mom. She gave me a solid gold ring with a red stone in it right after you left on the school bus, and she said it was treasure and she trusted me to guard it because I was her little man. And I wasn't supposed to go to the pirate swamp alone while you were away at school, but I went anyhow that one day because I had to bury the treasure real quick before it got lost or stolen or something."

Nathan gave a hard jab and the little rock came loose and bounced out of the hole. It rolled close to my knee and I stared at it, stunned, wondering what to ask next.

"Whuh . . . why are we just now digging up this ring, Nathan? Why didn't you dig for it years ago?"

He ran his arm across his sweaty forehead, leaving grime. "I kind of forgot about it till lately. After we sell the ring for a million dollars, I hope we can use five bucks to hire a detective to find my rabbits."

He started digging again, so hard and furiously I thought he'd break my scissors. My chest ached and I had to bite my bottom lip hard and concentrate on my own digging.

I didn't believe there was a ruby ring, of course. On the other hand, the way he sounded so sure of his facts was eerie, and I could certainly see how having three operations and spending months in the hospital would make you forget things in the normal world, even treasure you'd just buried.

●　　●　　●

We didn't dig too much longer that afternoon because the plastic spoon broke.

But I went back out with him the next afternoon. I even agreed to take my potato-carving knife for one of us to dig with while the other one used my scissors.

I was supercooperative because I wanted to ask him more sneaky questions.

Like the day before, I waited till we'd been digging for half an hour or so, then sat back on my heels, fanned my face with my hand, and tried to sound casual.

"Nathan, do you think Jack knew that Mama had that treasure ring she told you to guard?"

"Yeah," Nathan said immediately. "He knew all right."

I laughed a little to hide how flabbergasted I was by his quick answer. "Oh, yeah? What makes you so sure about that?"

Nathan began bouncing the point of the scissors in the bottom of his hole, poking at the dirt faster and faster. "Because of the thing he said to me one second before my legs got crunched that afternoon."

I froze for about a full minute, too shocked to think, then I leaned closer to him. "Nathan, I didn't think you remembered anything about the accident," I said.

"I just started remembering things when Jack decided to sell my rabbits. Now it's sort of like a scary movie that I can't make stop. Right one second before my legs got crunched, I remember Jack said, 'Now, if you just keep still, this will be our last afternoon before good times.' See, Jack and Mom wanted me to keep the treasure secret and safe because they were going to sell it the next day to give us good times. But I got crunched and couldn't tell where it was, so now Jack hates me."

"Jack doesn't hate you, Nathan," I whispered back.

Nathan looked at me so innocently I couldn't stand it. "Sure he does," he said. "That's why he sold my rabbits."

I needed to talk to my mother about this, but it was hard to know how to. I couldn't tell her we were digging out at The Penitentiary, for starters. And though I was sure there wasn't a ruby ring, if there was, where would *she* have gotten it? Since she'd never mentioned it to me, it didn't seem like something I could ask her about.

After everybody else was in bed that night, except for Jack, who hadn't been around all weekend, I went into the kitchen where she was sitting, filing down the spark plugs.

"Nathan thinks Jack hates him. He thinks that because Jack sold his rabbits," I said.

She stopped filing and just stared at me for a few seconds. Then she blew on the spark plug to clear away the little metal slivers. "That's ridiculous," she said.

I shrugged. "I'm just telling you what Nathan thinks."

She put down the file and spark plug and sat there staring at the refrigerator with her mouth open a little bit. There were little worry lines between her eyebrows. Anyway, that's what they looked like to me. Worry lines, like they talk about in face cream commercials.

14 • WHAT IS ART?

Miss Valentino says art is the way humans express their most intimate and passionate desires and dreams.

My mother says art should look like something and go with your sofa.

Mrs. Peck says art tells a lot about the civilization that created it.

"Would you agree, Miss Capperson?" she asked me Monday afternoon, my second day of work.

"Huh? I mean, what?" I was pulling weeds from around her yellow roses, and to be honest, I'd been listening to the wind more than to her. I just couldn't get over the way the wind up on her hill was always swishing through her garden like it was trying to dance with you, or whispering mysterious secrets to you when you were coming up the lane.

"Would you agree with the hypothesis I've just stated, that art can tell one a lot about the civilization that creates it? You *did* say when we first met that you're an art lover, did you not?"

"Yes," I pushed out.

"In fact, I believe your exact statement was, 'I just love art. All art.'"

I crouched there pulling those weeds, feeling my face start to burn. Why had I *said* such a stupid-sounding thing? I hadn't even seen one-one-*billionth* of the art that was around in different places, so how could I possibly know if I loved all of it?

"In fact," she said, straightening up and pushing one gardening glove into the small of her back, "that statement so impressed me that I determined that very instant to hire you as my personal assistant. What a pleasant surprise it's been to find you also share my interest in floriculture."

She hadn't just hired me for the *carpe diem*? She was actually . . . impressed? *Floriculture,* I said in my mind, just to hear it again.

"I'll help you with your flowers for free, Mrs. Peck. You don't have to pay me for the time we spend out here in the garden, just for the reading time, okay?"

"Nonsense. As we agreed, you'll be paid for two hours of your valuable time, three afternoons a week—Monday, Wednesday, and Friday. We'll strive for a balance of reading, gardening, and conversation. Above all things, the ancient Greeks valued balance in their lives. Clarity and balance, as perfectly exemplified by their architecture."

"You mean those white buildings with all those columns," I said. Conversation with . . . me? "Miss Valentino has this book in the art room that shows those buildings, and they're just so beautiful I could cry. My favorite one is the Temple of Apollo at Delpie."

"Delphi," Mrs. Peck corrected. "And yes, I understand your reaction to those wonderful buildings and share it completely, Destiny. There was a famous oracle at Delphi, you know. People came from all over the world to ask her questions and they trusted completely in the answers she gave."

"My brother has a dead alligator snapping turtle that gives him answers like that," I told Mrs. Peck.

"Does he indeed?" she answered, nodding.

"And I've . . . I've been wanting to tell you, Mrs. Peck. I just love your garden statues. I just love them. Especially the one of the blindfolded girl holding up the two hanging birdbaths."

"That's Themis, Destiny. The goddess of justice and the law. The Romans put great stock in the law, and we've inherited much of our legal system from them. Themis is holding out a scale, and she's blindfolded because justice should be blind and everyone, king and pauper, treated fairly and equally under the law. And isn't it just dandy that those scales catch the rain so that the little chickadees and finches get a perfect splash spot?"

• • •

My mother and Bert and Ethelene were all crying when I got home that afternoon. Bert and Ethelene were standing in the playpen, whimpering and flinging their bodies against the sides. Nathan was in the kitchen making a whole assembly line of bologna sandwiches. My mother was pacing the floor with her coat on and dark mascara streaks where tears were streaming down her face.

"I don't know why you can't be here when I need you!" she sob-screamed at me.

"I was at work."

"Well some things are just a little bit more important than that dumb job of yours, such as your stepfather being in jail, for instance!"

Usually I would have pointed out that Jack wasn't my stepfather, that we only called him that in public. And she would have pointed out back that if you could get married and still get enough food stamps he probably would be. But that day I just said, "Jack's in jail? In jail for what?"

"They say him and Earl and some guys burned down a restaurant Saturday night. They got the owner in jail for insurance fraud, and he says he paid Jack and Earl and some guys to actually do it. So now that you finally decide to come ambling on home to stay with the kids, I got to get down there on the double to be Jack's alibi so the police will just quit their endless picking on him and leave us alone for a huge change!" She sniffled and added, "It's just darn lucky I got the truck running this afternoon, that's all I can say."

She yanked open the front door and fluttered out. I picked her purse up from the sofa and ran after her with it, but she was already in the truck, looking frantically for her keys, which were in her purse. "Don't worry, they won't pick on him!" I yelled through the slitted truck window as I crammed her purse through. "Everybody gets fair and equal treatment under our legal system, which we inherited from the Romans themselves."

"Ha! Get real, Dess. What planet you been living on?" she yelled back. Then she found her keys, started the truck, and peeled from the driveway.

• • •

"Bologna is made from pigs," Nathan said when the four of us were eating his too-mustardy sandwiches a while later. "The wrapper says so."

Ethelene was eating her sandwich from the middle out. She suddenly stuck her nose through the hole she'd nibbled and let the sandwich dangle from her face, expecting us all to be impressed. Only Bert laughed.

"Stop that, Ethelene," I said. "Eat right. You're being babyish."

"Shup, idjit!" she ordered. "You idjit you."

"And don't say shut up and idjit. It's *not* funny, especially coming from a big girl like you."

"Hamburgers are made from cows," Nathan said.

"Nathan?" I took a deep breath. "I didn't see Jack anywhere around Saturday night, did you? He wasn't around all weekend, was he?"

Nathan stiffened, like he did lately when anyone mentioned Jack. Then he said, "Food is made from *big* animals, not little animals."

I might as well say what he needed to hear and get it over with. "I think somebody might have bought the rabbits for pets," I told him. "Probably somebody did that."

It wasn't easy, telling such a whopper to his face like that. People only bought cute pet store bunnies for pets, not big old fat and sluggish rabbits like Nathan's. Rabbits like Nathan's were bought to skin, fry, and eat. Period.

15 • SHAPES

Jack came home with our mother late that night. I have to admit I was hoping he wouldn't, because now I knew we'd make our usual Tuesday potato run.

Art I that Tuesday turned out to be sort of depressing, too. Miss Valentino had replaced the wonderful things she'd yanked off her French bulletin board last Thursday with plain old shapes in bright colors. A circle, a triangle, a square, a trapezoid, a hexagon, an octagon.

"Who can identify this shape?" she asked, pointing to the circle.

No one raised a hand. Finally, Samantha did and Miss Valentino called on her.

"It's, like, a circle?" Samantha said.

"Yes!" Miss Valentino said. "Now, who can identify this one?" She pointed to the square.

For a long time no one raised a hand. Finally, Samantha did, and Miss Valentino called on her, but chewed her bottom lip, smiling but obviously disappointed. I started wishing I'd raised my hand, though I usually saved that for when the questions were hard, or at least not kindergarten-level.

"It's, like, a square?" Samantha said.

Miss Valentino nodded and pointed to the trapezoid and said, "Can anyone who's not already answered a question this afternoon identify this shape for us?"

Without raising his hand, Russell said, "It's a triangle with the top whacked off."

Everybody just sat there. It would have been less depressing if they'd laughed or something.

I raised my hand and said it was a trapezoid, but I could tell it didn't make Miss Valentino feel that much better.

She quickly pointed to the hexagon and octagon and said their names herself, then told us to work on our own projects the rest of the hour. Which meant the boys drew vicious comic book heroes and most of the girls wrote notes to each other.

I took out the picture of the Eiffel Tower I'd rescued from her floor last week and began doing some sketches of how I might be able to make a real one.

• • •

Jack was sort of sick on the potato run, hungover, I expect, from his big weekend. And he was really angry besides about being arrested.

"I should sue," he kept grumbling between belches and moans. "If it wasn't for Virginia vouching for me, I'd still be sitting in that jail having my rights violated."

I had my own problems and didn't give him one bit of sympathy. Lugging those potatoes up to people's doors was totally awful that day. You could now tell from several feet away that the potatoes were rotten. I even considered just faking my sales and giving Jack the whole eight dollars I had earned so far from two days of work for Mrs. Peck. In fact, I *did* sort of warn most of the people not to buy.

"You don't need to take any potatoes since they may possibly not be fresh this particular week, but would you mind just opening the sack and looking at them?" I whispered to Mrs. Baker and Mrs. Houston and a few others, adding in my mind, *so if Jack is watching he won't be all over my case for not selling hard enough.*

Nobody at all took potatoes, and practically everybody gave me the same money as usual, though most of them gave Jack a dirty look while they did it. Dirty looks he didn't see, since he's always slumped down so far when he waits in the truck.

Mrs. Nichols asked me to give a message to my mother. She told me to tell her that she was sorry she'd caught her at a bad time the other night, and that she was still hoping to stop by someday soon and have a little longer chat because the new high school equivalency class was starting soon.

I wiped off the window and looked toward the willow trees as we drove away from Mrs. Nichols's house. Samantha and Crystal and Rachel were skipping around and waving their arms in the air, playing something new. They had colored wands with long streamers in their hands, and they must have made them themselves because some of the streamers were falling off every time they waved them around.

Those decorated Barbie parts shoeboxes they carried around with them weren't much better, to tell the truth. They'd tried to draw Barbies on the lids, but they looked like huge bowling pins with fluffy hair and blue eyes.

I'm sorry, but they are just *not* that good at art.

•　•　•

I took my duct tape to school the next day. I wasn't sure Rachel and Samantha and Crystal would have enough nerve to play their babyish wand game at recess, but they did. I also wasn't sure I'd have enough nerve to just go up and offer to help them with their superlame wands, but I did.

"You'd have better luck keeping the streamers on those wands if you used duct tape," I said when I reached them. "You could get some glitter from Miss Valentino to make them look more magical and artistic, too."

Rachel glowered at me. "What's duct tape? That stuff around your wrist?"

I was wearing the duct tape roll as a bracelet. "Here, I'll show you," I said, tearing off a six-inch piece of tape with my teeth. A little to my surprise, Crystal poked her wand out, and I wrapped the tape where the streamers were barely attached by an ugly ball of plain old cellophane tape. The duct tape worked even better than I'd thought it would. The streamers not only were on more solidly, but they looked perky, sort of like the wand was wearing a grass skirt. And the duct tape shone like silver.

"Huh!" Samantha sounded impressed. "Do me!"

"What are you playing now, anyhow?" I asked as I bit off another piece of tape and wound Samantha's wand.

"Fairy godmothers," Rachel answered. "Samantha's stuffed dinosaur is Sleeping Beauty, and we're her good fairy godmothers. We protect her and give her good gifts. If you want to be the bad fairy godmother, you can, since you cuss. You could come running up on us cussing and give Sleeping Beauty some kind of obnoxious gift, then we could chase you away, then you could get mad and cuss at Sleeping Beauty."

"I only cussed that once," I said. "And anyway, I don't have a wand."

• • •

I glanced into the art room on my way to lunch. Miss Valentino was sitting at her desk eating corn chips. When she saw me she smiled and waved for me to come in.

"Have a chip," she said, tilting the bag toward me. "How do you like the new bulletin board, Destiny? Basic shapes and primary colors. Clean and simple, just like my teaching and my whole life are going to be from now on. Uncomplicated."

I nibbled my chip and looked over at the bulletin board again. I just couldn't lie about it. "No offense, Miss Valentino, but I miss the hayfields and foggy bridges and ladies in white dresses. I always thought the Eiffel Tower in the middle of all those pictures looked like a spider in a magical dream web."

She nodded, but she almost seemed sad again, like after class last Thursday. "To be honest, Dess, I should add a blue diamond and a yellow triangle, but I can't get up one bit of enthusiasm for doing it. By the way, how's the new job going?"

"Fine," I said. "Miss Valentino? Can I ask you a question? Do you think people can sort of . . . go bad? I mean, like a potato that is fine in August and September, but gets rotten in late October from being in there with another bad potato for too long a time?"

"Wow, Destiny, that's a heavy question. You mean, can a living person just start to . . . rot, over time? Physically?"

I took a deep breath, thinking. "I don't mean physically. I mean like . . . actions. Can a person's actions just start to go bad on her without her even knowing it, so that when people stop ignoring her and start to notice her they mostly just *expect* her to do bad things? And then suddenly she's doing them? Like, let's say . . . cussing?"

She sat there chewing slowly and frowning, thinking. "Could happen, I guess," she said. "An artist, for instance, misunderstood for years might just . . . snap and do wild things. Take van Gogh cutting off his ear. Of course, that could have been craziness from lead poisoning because of all that paint he kept getting in his mouth."

I nodded. "Also, could I borrow a little more red glitter, Miss Valentino?"

16 • CRONUS RULES

After nearly a week of knowing her, I was still afraid of Mrs. Peck. I kind of figured I always would be. She was just that kind of person. After all, Miss Valentino had said even her principal had been afraid of her.

But on the bus to her house that afternoon, I realized, afraid or not, I was looking forward to seeing her. I liked the way she talked to me about the Romans and those Greek buildings. I liked the way she just let me figure out what floriculture was without explaining it. Sometimes she corrected my pronunciation when I read to her, but she did it in a snappy, no-nonsense way, then let it go. I was careful to pronounce that word right the next time, and she seemed to know I would, so she didn't just lie in wait trying to catch me doing it wrong again.

When I got to the top of her wonderful lane that

afternoon, it took me a while to find her. I looked in the flower garden, and then I knocked on her door. I hadn't been in her backyard either of my other two workdays. I went around the side of the house to look there next, holding my breath and tiptoeing for some reason.

It was beautiful back there, in a wild and less organized way than in the front. There were flowers everywhere, but these were shaggier varieties—mostly daisies and red poppies. There was a goldfish pond, with birdhouses hanging from the trees that surrounded it.

She was sitting on a little stone bench down the hill and far in the distance. Her back was to me. I thought about yelling to her, but the way she was sitting so straight and quietly made me decide to walk down to her instead.

"Mrs. Peck?" I whispered when I got close.

"I've been awaiting your arrival, Miss Capperson," she said without turning to me. She had a book on her lap, partly covered with her folded hands. "Sit here beside me. I thought we might read in the sunshine today. We'll have few enough beautiful days like this from now on. Old Cronus will soon be ushering in the winter."

"Cronus?"

"The Greek god of time, similar to the god called Saturn by the Romans. He was perhaps the most powerful of the elder gods. Time, you see, rules all things."

She put up one hand to shade her eyes. "This is my

favorite spot on the property. Can you see the river beyond that hedge at the bottom of the hill?"

I looked. "Yes." You could see for miles.

She opened the book to a page she had marked with a photograph. "Cronus, or Saturn, was one of a race of giants known as Titans. Themis, the goddess of justice whom we discussed the other day, was another. The Greeks believed the Titans ruled the earth in the very beginning, before the latter gods came along and took their place. Another of the Titans was named Prometheus, and to him and his brother Epimetheus had fallen the job of creating Mankind."

She handed the open book to me. "I began to learn mythology when I was somewhat younger than you are now, Destiny. As a child, I lived several months a year at the home of my uncle Milton, who was a professor of the classics. My parents were anthropologists, you see, and often gone doing fieldwork overseas. Uncle Milton was a bachelor. I don't imagine he much enjoyed the company of a young girl like me. I was ten years old, I think, when he charged me to read the story we'll read today from this very same book. He told me to ponder it well, which I promised to do. I'm not at all sure I knew what 'ponder' meant, but I was a rather nervous child and I tried in all things and at all costs to be quiet and obedient, you see."

I smiled, but I felt sad thinking of Mrs. Peck as a little girl, alone and scared in some house with this uncle who didn't like her much. "Should I start reading now?" I asked.

"If you please," Mrs. Peck answered, and closed her eyes.

The story was called "Prometheus and Pandora," and it turned out to be pretty exciting. The first part was about those two Titans she'd mentioned, Prometheus and Epimetheus. Besides his job of creating Mankind, Epimetheus was supposed to give each animal a special thing it could use to survive. So he gave the lion courage, the birds wings—you get the picture. The trouble was, he messed up big-time by using everything up and not saving something wonderful to give to Man. His brother Prometheus got the big idea of going up to the chariot of the sun and bringing down fire. This gift of fire made Man superior to all the other animals, *but* it made the chief god of the heavens, Zeus, mad, mad, mad. So Zeus made the very first woman, Pandora, to punish the Titans and Man both for stealing from the heavens.

"What do you think about the story so far?" Mrs. Peck asked when I got to that part.

"I think it's pretty darn insulting to us girls," I answered.

She nodded. "My generation of females wouldn't have taken offense, at least not openly. But perhaps we should have. Read on, please."

Epimetheus had this sealed jar in his house that

contained all the bad stuff he'd had left over when he gave those good traits to all the animals. Well, he warned Pandora to keep her hands off it, but she was just way too curious. One day she opened the lid of the jar a teeny-weeny bit, and all those bad things flew out and took root in the world. Everything from sicknesses to meanness to just plain pure evil got out of that jar because of Pandora and her stupid nosiness.

When I got that far, Mrs. Peck reached over and quietly took the book from me.

"As you can imagine, Destiny, I didn't touch any of Uncle Milton's fusty old bachelor possessions after this story, which was surely his hope when he ordered me to 'ponder' it." She smiled, and leaned sideways to whisper, "Of course, I never found anything remotely interesting about his smelly old cigar boxes or the desk drawers where he stashed his rum in the first place."

I smiled back. "I think we should read to the end, Mrs. Peck. There's another couple of pages."

"Let's go work on the roses right now while the light is still good. You can finish the story on your own at home tonight."

"You'll lend me the book?" My ears were ringing. I couldn't believe she'd let a book this old and beautiful out of her sight. The edges were gold and everything.

"Of course. You can finish the story in bed tonight, and between now and then you can enjoy that most delicious of feelings—anticipation."

• • •

When I got home that afternoon, I stood for a few seconds on our tiny porch with my hand on our doorknob, wondering what kinds of bad things were going to fly out at me after I shoved open the front door.

At first I thought that nothing did. When I opened the door there was no blaring TV laughter, no howling, no wet diaper smell, no Jack yelling at people to shut up, no anybody calling anybody else idjit, no Mama talking in a desperate voice to Helena, no Nathan rampaging or anything. It was quiet.

Way *too* quiet. "Mama? Nathan?"

I checked upstairs and downstairs. My mother and my two sisters were gone. Jack was definitely nowhere around. I finally happened on Nathan in the kitchen, drawing a picture of a rabbit in one corner of the arithmetic paper he was working on.

"Nathan! Why didn't you answer me? Where *is* everybody?"

"They're at jail," he said without looking up. "The cops came and got them."

"You . . . saw the police come in and take our whole family to jail?"

He nodded, shoved his bangs out of his eyes with his pencil, and went on drawing.

I asked him a bunch more questions, of course, but he just shrugged each time. He really didn't know anything except that while he'd been sitting here minding his own business, the police had come in and taken away our entire family.

All we could do was wait. I heated up some soup and made us some peanut butter sandwiches, and while we ate I told Nathan about how the rich Romans ate lying on couches and took baths in these huge swimming pools with lots of other people.

17 • ALL THE BAD THINGS FLY OUT OF THE JAR

My mother came home in Jack's truck a while later, without Jack. She was wild-eyed as she kicked open the front door, stormed through the living room, and stomped up the stairs with one of my too-terrified-to-howl sisters under each arm.

Nathan immediately hid behind the sofa.

"Destiny Louise Capperson, you get upstairs this second to help me with these two filthy girls!" she screamed, and I ran upstairs, wishing I could hide with Nathan instead.

I kept my eyes down and didn't ask any questions while I worked on changing Bert's diaper and getting some of the ketchup off her face and hands. They must feed you in jail. Across the room, my mother was slamming one of Ethelene's drawers open and closed over and over again, yelling something I couldn't understand with each slam. While her back was turned like that, I crept quickly over and grabbed Ethelene from the floor where she had put her, then brought her over to Bert's part of the room to get her the rest of the way undressed and cleaned up. My mother picked up a brush from the floor, threw it at the wall so hard it cracked the plaster, then grabbed her hair in both hands and ran shrieking from the room.

I put the girls in their beds and they squiggled themselves into balls, trying their best to burrow right into their mattresses. "Everything's okay," I whispered to them as I turned off the light, wishing everything was.

•   •   •

My mother was still locked in her bedroom when it was time for me to go to school the next morning, so I got Nathan on the bus but I stayed home to take care of Bert and Ethelene. I had some time to start a new art project while they were still asleep, so I spread a grocery bag on the kitchen table and began painting the toothpicks I'd bought at the school store with the black tempera paint I keep around to paint my potato zebras.

My mother came into the kitchen when I had about two dozen toothpicks painted and about five dozen to go. She looked awful. Her face was puffy and her hair was matted, so every single dark root showed.

"Don't worry. I bought these toothpicks with my own money," I mentioned quietly.

"I feel lousy," she said. She pulled the empty coffee pot open and squinted into it, then threw it into the sink. She yanked the grocery bag we use for kitchen trash out from under the sink and started rooting through it until she found a cigarette butt that wasn't smoked clear down to the filter.

"That's gross," I informed her as she lit it. It wasn't the best time for me to be criticizing, but I just couldn't help pointing out that one thing.

She stood inhaling and looking out the window with her hand on her hip. Her fancy nails looked funny against the old green bathrobe she was wearing.

"Well, Destiny, in this life you do whatever it takes to get you through each day," she said without turning toward me. "That's what life *is* for a woman, doll. One lousy, stinking day strung on the tail of the one before it. Endless work and worry while the men you pin your sweet hopes on just . . ."

While I listened, I was also trying to crease the edge of the grocery bag so it would stick straight up and make a little wall I could lean my painted toothpicks against while they dried. The first ones I'd painted looked so smeary on the side that had been against the bag that I was afraid I'd have to do them over. "The men just what?" I asked, carefully balancing the first few toothpicks. "Is Jack in jail again or something?"

She threw the butt into the sink and turned to drop

into the chair across from me. She slumped with her chin in her right hand, and started aimlessly flicking my leaning toothpicks over with her left index finger.

"Stop it!" I yelled. "Those are *supposed* to be standing up like that!"

She heeled her chair back and threw her arms up. "Well, snap my head off why don't you, Miss Lah-de-dah? How was I supposed to know that? Just pretty please forgive me for even living, will you, Destiny? And while you're at it, forgive me for even bothering to *have* you, when I could have been going to my junior prom instead right about that time. And forgive me for even marrying your father, who disappeared the most completely of any of them. Could you do that for me pretty please, Miss Smart Aleck?"

I began arranging the toothpicks against their little wall again as I said, "You could have assumed if someone is taking the trouble and time to do something that you're not supposed to just . . . undo it, whether you know what it is or not." My voice was shaking.

"Fine," she said, and kicked the table leg so hard the toothpicks fell again.

"Stop it!" I yelled again, and this time I was crying. "You *did* have me and you have to *think* about things! You had me and Nathan and Ethelene and Bert, and now you can't just keep saying you don't want to think about anything! You *have* to!"

Grabbing up the toothpicks, I ran out of the kitchen and up to my studio, where I cried so hard I cried myself to sleep.

· · ·

My cheek was stuck to the rubber of the air mattress when Ethelene and Bert woke me up, calling me. Groggily, I dressed them both. I just couldn't face going downstairs, and they were both overdue for an art lesson anyway.

"We're going to create the Eiffel Tower as a gift for Miss Valentino," I told them. "And I want you to pay close attention to instructions, because I don't feel like repeating things a jillion times today."

Ethelene reached for the scissors, and I put my knee on them.

"Cut!" she bellowed.

I sighed. "You can be the cutter, but first I have to tell you how. See, we have to make little X's out of all these black toothpicks. Your job will be to cut each toothpick in half so we'll have enough." I pointed to Miss Valentino's thrown away Eiffel Tower picture, which I'd taped to the wall. "The Eiffel Tower looks like a tall, cartoony upside-down V, and most of the V is made of black X's."

"*THHHHHHH!*" Bert said, flapping her arms and nodding.

I showed Ethelene how to hold the scissors in two hands so she could get enough grip to cut clear through a toothpick. To my surprise, she did a great job. I lined up several toothpicks on the floor in front of her, and she clamped her tongue between her lips in concentration and carefully went after the exact middle of each one. Bert thought Ethelene was performing magic just for her amusement, and clapped her hands.

We worked like that for a while, Ethelene quietly concentrating on making perfect cuts, Bert breathlessly admiring Ethelene, me gluing the half-toothpicks into X's while trying to figure out if I could possibly cut big strips of black from one of the broken televisions in the yard to use as the frame of the V.

Were those TV's metal, or plastic?

I didn't even realize my murky sadness was gone until, suddenly, we heard our mother's yelling voice. I came out of my art trance with a stomach-turning jolt. My two little sisters swiveled their heads to stare at me, expecting me to . . . what?

"Well *finally* there you are, Helena."

She was on the phone, at least. Not yelling at someone face-to-face.

"Helena, I can't believe you haven't picked up all morning long. Me, sound *upset*? Well that *could* be because that slimeball that owns that burned-down restaurant I told you about is sticking to his story about Jack burning it, and they've got Jack under arrest again. Yesterday the police hauled him and me *both* in for questioning, and even though I took my little girls with me to make an impression, the officers kept hounding and hounding me anyway about how big-deal a thing it is to lie under oath. So now I've got the grand choice of ratting on my fiancé or letting my story stand about him being here last weekend and possibly getting to go to jail myself, how's that?"

"Go on cutting, Ethelene," I whispered. "Don't listen, just cut."

"I *will* pay you the ninety cents a minute I owe for the last few calls, Helena, but you know I can't till I get that big piece of luck you been promising me! Helena? Helena!"

We heard a jangly crashing sound that I was pretty sure was the phone sailing across the living room and hitting the wall.

"Shup?" Ethelene whispered, looking scared.

Bert started crying without making a sound. She just sort of puckered up her whole little face, turned red, and let go with the tears so quietly it was like TV with the mute button pushed.

I pulled one of them close with each of my arms and turned my back to our door like a shield. We stayed like that, hoping we didn't hear her coming up the stairs.

When I heard her bedroom door slam shut downstairs I nearly fainted with relief.

• • •

My mother says life is one stinking, lousy day strung on the tail of the one before it, but you have to remember she was in a bad mood when she said that.

Miss Valentino says life is going to be clean and uncomplicated for her from now on, but you have to remember she said that about her new primary shapes and colors bulletin board display, too, and it was so boring she didn't even finish putting it up.

I haven't heard Mrs. Peck's opinions about life, at least not in so many words.

Life. Life, life, life.

18 • THAT BIG PIECE OF LUCK

By that night, my mother was cried-out and quite a bit calmer. I made some hamburgers and took one to her bedroom. I knocked on her door.

"Come on in," she said in a hoarse voice. She was propped up in bed with her pillows behind her back and with some of her back issues of *Perfect Romance Magazine* strung around her. She reads those when she's upset because they put you in a different world. I understand that because I do art when I'm upset for the exact same reason.

She took the plate I held out and said, "Thank you, sweetheart. I appreciate your feeding the kids and looking out for them today. And I'm sorry I acted like an old poop when we were chatting in the kitchen this morning, too, okay?"

"Okay," I said as I sat down on the edge of the bed with my back to her. "Mama? I've been thinking. I have eleven dollars—by tomorrow afternoon I'll have fifteen. Would fifteen lottery tickets start us on the way to the big win Helena predicted? I mean, do you think it would take care of the part where you get enough for you and Ethelene to take the bus to California?"

I could tell by the way she chewed her burger that she was excited by the idea and trying not to be, both at once. Jack had never bought more than ten tickets at a time, even at our richest.

"That's your money, Destiny," she finally said. "You earned it and it's your own."

"But I'm not asking about that. I'm asking, would it *really* do the trick? Do you have a clear feeling that we'd win this time? If your deepest gut feeling is that Helena is right and we're on the verge of that big win, then if we *don't* put everything we've got into making it happen, couldn't the good luck just get jinxed because of our lack of faith?"

I'd given this a lot of thought this afternoon. A *lot*. If the problem was basically putting her sweet hopes in men, then having money enough to not have to do that ever again was surely the answer. And to get the ball rolling, we just *had* to have that big piece of luck Helena had been promising and promising.

In the dresser mirror, I saw my mother shake her head in this admiring way. "Destiny Louise, you are so smart. You've really thought this out, way better than *I* ever could."

I stared hard at our reflection there together. I tried to get up enough nerve to say the other thing I wanted to say, the thing I'd been rehearsing all afternoon.

"Did you really want to have me?" I finally pushed out.

I swallowed and looked down at my hands. My palms were blotchy and there were still traces of black paint in some of the calluses I had from gardening at Mrs. Peck's.

"Oh, Dess," she whispered. I heard her sniffling, so I looked into the mirror again. Her reflection looked back at me with sad eyes, and she crawled up and hugged me from behind.

•　　•　　•

Nathan helped me check the television sets in the yard right before it got dark that night. Most of them were metal, but one was plastic. Sometimes, things just work out so lucky it's nearly unbelievable.

I carefully drew the Eiffel Tower on the least dirty side of that plastic TV, then Nathan used my potato-carving knife to saw it out. He didn't do the neatest job in the world, but later, in my studio, I smoothed his ragged edges with scissors and made several small paper roses to glue over the worst places.

Just in case it still didn't look quite right to an expert like Miss Valentino, I decided to tell her it was also her initial if you held it upside down.

• • •

"I made something for you," I said when I put the Eiffel Tower on her desk right before school the next morning. "You can also use it for a V." I reached over her shoulder and turned it point-side down. "In this book Mrs. Peck lent me, all the chapters start with a real fancy first letter in the first word. And if you *want* to use it as the Eiffel Tower part of the time, you could just pretend those are giant roses planted in front of it."

Miss Valentino turned it back to Eiffel Tower position, then just kept staring down at it. Now that I could sort of see it through somebody else's eyes, I felt nearly sick with embarrassment. The TV plastic was faded brown instead of the grayish-black of the real Eiffel Tower. Also, the paint on some of the toothpicks was streaked and uneven, and those roses I'd cut out of a Marlboro wrapper I'd dug from the garbage were curling up at the edges and smelled, even from several feet away, like coffee grounds and nicotine.

"I think it looks better when it's a V," I mumbled.

Without looking at me, Miss Valentino said, "This is art, Destiny. You used artist's eyes to do this. You used an artist's heart. It's more France than France. It's the essence of France. It even smells like France, Destiny."

I could hardly breathe I was so thrilled by that compliment.

She turned to me and her chin was puckering.

"Thank you for this gift," she said. "It's about the most creative thing I've ever seen, and I'll always treasure it."

I didn't know what to say, so I just shrugged and said, "You love France."

"Yes," she said, in a whisper. "I guess a thing can't break your heart unless you love it."

•   •   •

Out on the playground, I thought more about that. Was my mother acting like her heart was broken by Jack, or only like her nerves were shot?

Crystal ran by me so close I felt the streamers on her wand tickle my arm.

"Don't you dare come into the castle and put a curse on our dear little Sleeping Beauty, you evil fairy godmother you!" she yelled at me over her shoulder.

So they still wanted me to play the cussing godmother. I didn't know whether to take that as a compliment or an insult, but since I was done with the Eiffel Tower anyway I decided my next project might as well be a really good wand.

19 • A NIP IN THE AIR

I agree with Mrs. Peck that anticipation is the most delicious of feelings. That's why I always try to have something to look forward to, especially when things are not going all that great. I hadn't finished "Prometheus and Pandora" either of the two nights I'd had it because it was the thing I was looking forward to. I decided I wouldn't let myself read it yet in case things got even worse at home. I'd hold back as long as I could.

But as I walked slowly up Mrs. Peck's beautiful lane that Friday afternoon, it occurred to me she would be expecting me to bring her valuable book back today. I was thinking about that and walking with my eyes closed so I could savor the sound of the magical overhead leaves when I almost got run over by a skinny bald man riding a green bicycle.

He was coasting down from the top of the lane

without pedaling, his pale and hairy bare legs stuck out to the sides. He was wearing black dress shoes and white socks, and the wind got inside the bottoms of his Bermuda shorts and blew them out like plaid balloons. "*Hel*-lo! *Hel*-lo! Heads up! Stand clear, please!" he called.

I scrambled out of his way. He smiled and saluted me as he whizzed on past, so I saluted back. I turned to watch him go on down the hill. He had some fuzzy red hair on the back of his head that blew straight out behind him like a soft little flame.

I hurried on up the lane then. Mrs. Peck was in the garden, but she wasn't working. She was just standing very straight and still, staring off into space.

"Mrs. Peck, I'm sorry but I didn't bring your book," I called out as I ran up to her. "I will Monday, I promise. Or I could bring it tomorrow, even."

It would be a long walk from our house, but I could.

"I've been considering making a gift of that book to you, Destiny," she said, still staring into the distance. Her voice sounded like she was thinking about something else.

I didn't know what to say. It would be too embarrassing to thank someone for something they weren't actually going to give you, and she couldn't really be *seriously* considering giving me that beautiful book. Could she?

"Did you run into Major Farnclay on the trail up?" she asked.

That had to be the bicycle man.

"He almost ran into *me*," I told her. "Then he saluted."

"Yes." She smiled. "Conrad is a retired army man. He salutes the birds and the flowers on occasion. Once I caught him saluting the garbage can before he put it out."

"I liked it, though," I said. "I like it when people do polite things."

She sort of snapped out of her trance then and looked over at me. "Well yes, so do I, Destiny. You're perfectly right. I sometimes fear courtesy is becoming a lost art."

That stopped me from asking what I was dying to ask, which was whether Major Farnclay was, like, her boyfriend or something. It might not have been courteous.

"Miss Capperson," she asked, "have you ever been deeply affected by a landscape, or a beautiful piece of sculpture, or a soaring passage in a book, and then had no one in the whole wide world to talk with about it?"

"Yes," I answered truthfully.

She nodded solemnly. "The late Mr. Peck was so much fun to talk to. Conrad isn't really much of a conversationalist, nor is he well-read. But he's got a sweet nature. He's always bringing me little gifts, most of them silly things I'll never find a use for. I tuck them away in a drawer in the house. In fact, he made me a present of a pair of garden snips we might well use today. Let's get them."

· · ·

When we were in the shadowy parlor of her house, she explained that garden snips were tiny scissors. She sat in one of her green velvet chairs across the room and waited for me to rummage them out of the little desk drawer where she stored Major Farnclay's gifts.

"He brought you *all* this stuff?" I asked.

"Yes, I believe the drawer was empty to start with. I've forgotten now exactly what all is in there. Anything interesting, would you say?"

"Well, there are several packages of Juicy Fruit gum, and there's a pearl necklace in a red velvet box. And there are a whole bunch of ink pens with different slogans on them, like they give you at the gas station and places. And there's a beautiful green mirror with a handle on it, and a box of chocolate candy, only it looks kind of whitish and hard, and there's a little calendar from three years ago, and a deck of playing cards in cellophane, and . . ."

I stopped. I could hardly believe my eyes.

"Mrs. Peck! There are five lottery tickets in here, fastened together with a rubber band! They haven't even been scratched!"

"Tickets, you say? Conrad bought tickets to somewhere?"

"*Lottery* tickets, Mrs. Peck! They sell them at the grocery store and you can get rich! My mother is buying some this very night. All you do is scratch off the numbers to see if you're a big winner."

"Destiny, does any of that chewing gum appear to be salvageable?"

I opened one of the gum packages and took out a piece. I could bend it, so I took it over to her. "Mrs. Peck, don't you want to scratch your tickets?"

"I doubt I could see to do it, much less tell if I'd won anything. Have a piece of gum, Destiny. Or shall we split this piece of mine?"

"Mrs. Peck? I could scratch off your tickets for you."

"As you wish, Destiny. Are those little snips in there anywhere, do you think?"

I found them and took them to her, and while she turned on the lamp beside her to closely inspect them, then turned off the lamp and made her way by touch across the room and back out to the porch, I quickly scratched the tickets.

• • •

"There's a nip in the air this afternoon," she was saying when I ran out to join her. We started down the wide porch stairs. "I've left a book on the garden swing, Destiny, but we'll leave ourselves time to cut the remaining roses. There may be a freeze tonight. Flora would be displeased with us if we let her children wither in the cold."

She looked over at me. "Destiny?"

"What, Mrs. Peck?"

"You seemed preoccupied. I expected you to display your usual lively curiosity when I alluded to the mythical Flora. Flora was the Roman goddess of flowers, you see. Pomona was goddess of the fruit trees. Faunus, grandson of the great Saturn himself, was the frolicsome god of the fields. He was a favorite of my late husband, Mr. Peck's. Many times as we landscaped this place, he'd put a finger to his lips and ask if I could not hear the laughter of Faunus."

We'd reached the garden swing. I sat down and picked up the book, but she kept standing, smiling sadly and looking across the fields. "I went to Rome to grieve when Mr. Peck died, and I grieve still after all these long twelve years," she finally said quietly.

The statue of Themis was near the garden swing. One of her scales was pulled way down and hanging sideways because it was clogged with soggy leaves. That made the other scale useless, too, since it was wedged way up against Themis's fingers where the birds couldn't stand on it. I left the book on the swing and walked over to start cleaning it up and balancing it.

"Mrs. Peck, remember when you told me there were lots of slaves to do the work and stuff in Rome? Would they have gotten the same fair and equal treatment by the law as, you know, the other kind of people? The regular citizens who were mostly rich?"

Mrs. Peck sat down in the swing and sighed. "Alas,

Destiny, no. Slaves had no rights under the law, which shall always stand as a black blot on the otherwise remarkable Roman legal system."

•   •   •

When we finished cutting the roses that chilly afternoon, she put them all into my arms and told me to take them home. *"Sic transit gloria mundi,"* she said. "Thus passes away the glory of the world."

On the city bus, I fanned the roses out on my lap and arranged them by color, white to deepest red, with all the shades of pink in between.

Once, I reached into my pocket and touched the lottery ticket. I thought it gave me a little electric shock, but that was probably my imagination.

I wasn't stealing it, just borrowing it for the weekend. I'd give it to Mrs. Peck on Monday. There just hadn't been a good time to explain the significance of it to her, sad and wistful as she'd been today about the weather and her dead husband. And besides, I wanted a closer, unrushed look at it. I'd never seen a $200 winner before. I'd never seen a $100 winner before. Once, Jack had scratched a $50 winner, and that had been pretty exciting. Nothing like the adrenaline rush I'd gotten when I scratched off that third matching $200 of Mrs. Peck's this afternoon, though.

Two of the white roses were still really just delicate buds, and I took them out of the lineup and set them aside to put in a separate vase for my sisters.

20 • GLAMOROUS HURRICANE VIRGINIA

When I got home, I went around to the back door and crept quietly into the kitchen so I could get the roses arranged in containers before anyone saw them. I found two empty coffee cans under the sink. The big bouquet looked wonderful, but the two little roses just listed to the side of their can. I finally found a ketchup bottle deep in the garbage sack that worked better for them. I was hoping to have time to wash the stickiness off it, but my mother came into the kitchen before I could get that far.

"Well, Destiny Louise, where in the world did you steal *those* from?"

She was smiling as she came over and buried her nose in the big bouquet, but still that comment struck me wrong.

"Why would you think I stole them?" I asked. "For your information, they were a gift, from Mrs. Peck."

She grabbed the biggest, reddest rose from the center of the bouquet, broke the stem off, and stuck it behind her ear. "Don't I look just *glah*-morous, darling?" She pursed up her lips and batted her eyes, doing a movie star imitation. "Look out, California surfer boys, Hurricane Virginia's about to hit your coast!"

I reached into my inside jacket pocket and handed her my fifteen dollars. "I had those roses all arranged," I said. "Now there's a hole in the middle."

"'Now there's a hole in the middle,'" she repeated in this high, silly voice as she took my dollar bills. "Snap out of it, Dess, and lighten up! We're gonna have faith, remember? Okay, now—the girls are in front of the TV and Nathan's somewhere. Unless there's a big line at the counter at Zimmer's Grocery, I should be back with the tickets in an hour at the most. You can start the macaroni if people get hungry, okay?"

"Okay," I said. I picked up the ketchup bottle and turned to the sink to wash it.

"Destiny Louise Capperson! Now you just shake off those gloomies and turn around here and give me a lucky smile this instant!"

I rolled my eyes, then turned and smiled at her. She was right—I could jinx this whole big win Helena had predicted if I didn't snap out of this strange gloomy mood.

"*That's* better," my mother said. She crossed her fingers on both hands and I crossed mine, too, then she blew me a lucky kiss and I blew her back a lucky kiss as she hustled from the kitchen. I heard her telling the girls something, and a few seconds later I heard the front door swoosh closed behind her.

The rose she'd broken off had fallen out of her hair and was on the floor over near the refrigerator. I went and picked it up, but she'd accidentally stepped on it and it was too mangled to use in the bouquet.

Ethelene came crawling into the kitchen, and I held the rose out to show it to her, thinking I might as well make fixing it into an art lesson.

"Ethelene, let me tell you something. Situations like this always make me wonder how any artist can survive without duct tape. You can hold things together with duct tape, such as mushy potatoes or poorly constructed magic wands. You can make shiny armor with it, like a knight would wear. I've made tons of swords and shields for Nathan out of cardboard and duct tape. You can stick duct tape along the edges of your drawings so your pictures are displayed in glittering silver frames. You can cut stars from it and attach them to the ceiling. And, of course, you can create the boundaries of a studio or the edges of a rabbit apartment building with it."

"Cut?" Ethelene got up on her knees, interested.

"Stand up and walk, Ethelene. Walk, and I'll let you help me fix this flower with some duct tape."

To my surprise, she actually got up and took a couple of steps toward me. I sat her in one of the kitchen chairs, went in and got Bert and put her in her high chair, and while we waited for the macaroni water to boil, Ethelene helped me reattach the broken rose to its stem with several layers of duct tape while Bert watched, her little mouth a straight line of concentration.

Nathan came wandering in while we were working.

"We didn't go digging all this week," he said, folding his arms and glaring at me.

"We'll try and go tomorrow or Sunday," I said. "But I'm not *promising,* okay?"

After we ate, I took the girls upstairs and got them ready for bed.

I put the bruised rose on my windowsill and before I knew what was happening, I went to sleep myself watching the moonlight caress its glowing silver stem.

● ● ●

"Twen-ty-se-ven dol-lars!" my mother announced the next morning. "Twen-ty-se-ven dol-lars, Destiny Louise!"

"That's how much we won?"

"That's our total from first-round play! We nearly doubled our money, Dess! Now, I'll take our winning tickets in and cash them for more tickets, and if we only hold a steady course we'll be in the four- or five-digit range in no time at all!"

All day Saturday, we went up slightly each time she went to Zimmer's and got new tickets. I think at our highest we'd won somewhere around sixty dollars.

But Sunday, we nose-dived fast. By lunchtime we were broke again.

My mother went into her room and closed the door, leaving all those tickets on the table half-buried in a rubbery gray sludge of scratched-off paint crumbs. I decided to collect the stubs and save them. I couldn't think of a use for them, but you never know.

It was when I was putting the stack of bright tickets into one of my art supply shoeboxes that I felt the strong urge to get Mrs. Peck's ticket out of my jacket pocket and bring it into my studio. I know what you may be thinking, but I was not tempted to exchange it with one of our loser tickets. I simply wanted to relive the thrill of seeing those three matching numbers, those $200's.

Stealing it didn't cross my mind until late that Sunday night, when everything in the entire world turned upside down.

21 • NIGHT CHANGES

It all started because of Mrs. Peck's beautiful book. Since all our dreams were as shriveled as that duct-taped rose on my windowsill, I realized Sunday afternoon that it was time to do the thing I'd been looking forward to. I plopped my sisters in their playpen and went upstairs, folded the top of my air mattress under to make a good reading pillow, then opened Mrs. Peck's beautiful book to the page in "Prometheus and Pandora" that was bookmarked by the photograph.

I slowly reread the list of awful things that had escaped from that jar when poor, curious Pandora opened it. A bunch of old-timey diseases—gout, rheumatism, colic. A bunch of mean emotions—envy, spite, revenge. For some reason, it was comforting to think of those bad emotions floating around where anybody at all could catch them like a cold. I guess I'd kind of thought they were like yelling and money worries and mostly just hung out in the houses of certain kinds of people.

I read on and found out that there was one thing left in the jar, hunkering way down in the bottom. That thing was "hope."

The idea took my breath away, like the ending of any really good story does.

Hope. I put the book on my stomach and just lay there thinking about it and looking at the ketchup bottle with the two pinkish-white roses I'd put by Ethelene's bed.

I was so lost in my thoughts that I didn't hear Nathan clumping up the stairs until he was nearly to the top. "I want to go digging right now!" he announced.

"Nathan, you know we can't leave the girls here alone when Mama's in a really blue mood like this. I'm going to read to you and that's that."

I sat up and pointed in a no-nonsense way to a spot on the air mattress right beside me, and, still glowering, he flopped down onto it and even leaned against me a little.

I found a story I'd noticed earlier about Herakles, the half-human son of Zeus, who had to do these twelve gross things that involved monsters. We read for a long time, longer than he'd ever let me read to him before. We read our way right out of our house and into ancient Greece.

When we stopped, it was dark. I yawned and reached

for the photograph to mark our place. "I think Mrs. Peck will let me keep the book longer, so tomorrow we'll . . ."

And that's when everything turned upside down.

Nathan jumped up, his face white and his eyes wide and dark. He began trembling.

My own heart slammed and I looked all around me for a poisonous snake or something. "What? Nathan, *what?*"

"It's . . . the *bad* lady!" he screamed, pointing to the photograph I had in my hand.

"This? No, Nathan, this is just Mrs. Peck when she was in Rome."

"She crunched my legs! Get her *away* from me!"

Things began swirling, like Pandora had opened that jar right in my face and all those awful things had gone straight up into my brain. The bad lady who had driven her car into Jack and Nathan's car and then driven away so heartlessly that day *couldn't* be Mrs. Peck!

Clutching the beautiful book, I ran down the stairs. My mother was sitting on the couch with the girls on each side of her. The TV wasn't turned up loud enough to hear, but she was staring listlessly at the screen.

I held the photograph in front of her nose. "Is this the bad lady that crunched Nathan's legs, yes or no?" I asked.

She gasped and put her hands over her mouth. "Where'd you get that awful thing?"

"I've got to go somewhere!" I pretty much yelled, and

I was out the front door before I could hear what she said back.

• • •

It was a damp and windy night, darker than usual because the moon was as skinny as it gets. I ran in the direction of Mrs. Peck's house and finally reached the tree-lined road with all the shining mailboxes. The cedar trees at the bottom of her lane were thrashing around like gladiators, trying to keep me back, but I dove between them anyway and ran on up the hill without letting myself stop.

The leaf canopy, so frilly and light in the daytime, at night seemed heavy and restless and spooky. As I plunged out into the clearing at the top of the lane, I felt pointed tree fingers snatch at my back, only missing by inches.

At the edge of the garden I stopped to get my breath, squeezing the book to my chest with both arms. The flowers were writhing in panic, like they'd just realized they were trapped with their feet in the dirt and it was nearly winter, the killing time. What god had Mrs. Peck said pulled things into the cold, underground darkness? A god with the name of a cartoon dog. Pluto, that was it.

"Stop thinking scary thoughts," I ordered myself, and I started walking, one foot then the other foot, toward the house. Leftover summer fireflies twinkled like bright eyes in the grass, and an owl called out. The ground felt spongy as quicksand.

124

"Mrs. Peck?" I yelled, running to the bottom of the stone porch steps.

I had no idea what time it was. She was probably asleep.

The house loomed darker than the sky. A gust of wind came around a pillar, shrieking.

I ran up the stairs and hammered on the door. "Mrs. Peck! Mrs. Peck!"

An aluminum garden chair went tumbling off the edge of the porch with a skeleton clatter. "Destiny?"

Mrs. Peck was suddenly standing in the doorway, ghostlike in a long white nightgown.

"Yes, it's me, Mrs. Peck! I came to, uh, give you back your book!"

"Destiny?" she repeated, holding the door wider open. "My, it's quite late and a very rough night for such an errand. Do your parents know you've come?"

"I only have a parent, not parents, and she doesn't much care what I do!" I was yelling partly out of nervousness and partly to be heard above the gusty wind. "I read some other stuff in your book besides Pandora, Mrs. Peck! I read, for instance, about the Furies and how they had snakes for hair and flew around hurting people who had done some secret crime and not been punished for it!"

I could actually hear my heart above the wind, it was beating so hard. Mrs. Peck kept standing there in her old-timey nightgown with her white hand on the doorknob and her hair weirdly glowing in the faint moonlight. She looked directly at me with her ruined eyes as though seeing clear through to my deepest thoughts, but she didn't take the bait and confess to any awful unpunished crime.

"I remember the first afternoon I worked for you, you said the pleasure of reading had been denied to you by some avenging Fury, Mrs. Peck! I was kind of wondering why you'd say a thing like that!"

"Will you come in?" Mrs. Peck asked.

When I yelled no thank you, she closed her eyes and tilted her head as though listening for something, then said, "Ah, yes, you're right. It's the kind of mysterious, blustery night that pulls one outside, into the elemental world."

She stepped through the doorway and crossed the porch, feeling her way with her long, bare feet. I didn't want to make her fall, but the second she reached the top step and settled herself down on it with her gown all around her like spilled milk, I blurted, "I mean . . . did you do some awful secret crime to someone, Mrs. Peck?"

She jerked a little and clutched her knees, sitting straighter, so straight it was like an electric current was going through her.

"You ask this because of your interest in the ancient concept of retributive justice, Destiny?" she asked after a while.

"I just asked because I want to understand, Mrs. Peck!"

For a few more seconds, she just kept sitting there like some ancient stone statue. The animals in the woods yipped and screamed and moaned.

"I feel we trust each other and I respect your intelligence, Destiny," she said, moving one hand to the concrete. "Come sit beside me and ask what you really want to know."

I stepped near her but didn't sit like she'd told me to.

"Mrs. Peck, did you run into a little boy with your car one day and crunch his legs?"

She immediately jerked up straighter, *too* straight, like people in Nathan's movies did when they took a knife to the stomach.

She put her hands over her mouth, just like my mother had done when I'd shown her the picture. Then she folded them and pressed them under her chin.

"That young boy's legs," she whispered with her eyes closed.

I began backing away from her, first slowly, then faster.

She stood up.

"Destiny? Destiny, stop!"

But I didn't. I kept backing away like that, faster and faster, until suddenly I was stopped by something hard and solid. It was the statue of Themis. I heard the chains of those two birdbaths clattering wildly against each other and I whirled around and caught the swaying goddess just as she was about to fall face forward to the ground.

"Please, Destiny, come back!" Mrs. Peck was calling. It seemed to me there were things swirling all around her back there on the porch, obnoxious things moving too fast to see clearly, things moaning and laughing at once and pulling at her gown and yanking her hair so she looked like a snaky-haired monster herself.

"No!" I screamed to Mrs. Peck, using every bit of my strength to shove teetering Themis back onto her stiff white feet.

22 • Mrs. Peck's Reader

I don't think I slept that night. I just kept lying there on my air mattress, looking at the windowsill where the lottery ticket was propped against the shriveled rose. Mrs. Peck had crunched my brother's legs. She was the bad lady and that was just that.

In the morning, I took the winning two-hundred-dollar lottery ticket downstairs and listlessly dropped it onto the kitchen table.

"What's this?" Mama asked, turning from where she'd been staring out the window over the sink. "And where'd you go last night, anyhow? Don't you just go running off like that, Destiny, you hear me?"

I flopped onto a kitchen chair and put my head down on my folded arms. I didn't feel so good. I heard her pick up the ticket.

"Oh, Destiny, oh. Oh, oh. Oh, oh, *oh!*"

Her squeals were making me even queasier. "It must have gotten mixed up in the ones you were throwing away," I muttered. "I mean, you must have read it wrong when you scratched it. Or something."

"I *knew* it, I *knew* it, I *knew* it!"

She ran out of the kitchen. I figured she was going to call Helena, and sure enough, I heard her squealing and laughing on the phone a few seconds later.

I scrunched my eyes tighter shut and pressed them against my arm.

•   •   •

At school I just kept feeling worse and worse. I don't have art on Mondays, but I stopped by to see Miss Valentino for a second after lunch.

She was cutting something out of construction paper for her next class. She glanced over at me and smiled. "So, do you approve of the *new* new bulletin board display?"

I looked. All the basic shapes were gone, and my Eiffel Tower project was right in the center of the bulletin board, with lots of Impressionist paintings mounted on all sides. All the circling black crows in those paintings suddenly reminded me of . . . Furies.

She put down the scissors and came over and took my shoulders in her hands. "Oh, Destiny, I'm so glad you stopped by, because I need to thank you. When I was in Paris last summer, I made spending money by sketching people who passed by on the sidewalk outside the room I rented. I could have done that this fall, too, but what I *really* wanted more than anything was to come home and be a teacher instead. But then when you gave me that Eiffel Tower that was also my initial, it was . . . it was almost like a sign, telling me a different direction to take. And so I thought about it all weekend, and I haven't told Principal Hyatt yet, but I'm quitting at semester to move back to France and live the poor but *glamorous* life of a street artist!"

I began shaking my head in horror and disbelief. I just couldn't help it. For one thing, that word "glamorous" reminded me of my mother, glamorous Hurricane Virginia, breaking the rose and buying those loser tickets. And there was another, more important thing—how could I get along without Miss V? Especially now.

"Don't you like being a teacher?" I asked with someone else's croaky, pathetic voice.

She squeezed my shoulders. "Be happy for me, Destiny!"

I tried to put together a smile, but I'm not so sure it looked that convincing. "Miss Valentino?" I asked. "What . . . what would be your definition of 'hope'?"

"Hope? Hope. Hope is . . . *carpe diem!* Hope is seizing every single day and living happily every single minute of your life without problems or disappointments!"

I nodded, tried again for a smile, and went on to class.

• • •

I had just assumed Mrs. Peck and I were through for good and I wouldn't go to my job after school, which is why I was surprised to find myself getting onto bus 4. When I got off at Mrs. Peck's mailbox, I stood there wondering what I thought I was doing. Then, still without knowing, I just started walking up the lane.

Yellow leaves had fallen to the ground during the weekend, and sunshine was oozing through the leaf canopy more than usual. In the garden, red and yellow rose petals were strewn all over the place like jewels.

There were dozens of birds clustered in the air around Themis's head, so many you expected her to angrily rip off that blindfold and start batting them away with it. As I got closer, I saw that the birds were frustrated because their little splash ponds were gone. The chains of the two scales had gotten completely tangled together and were now wrapped around Themis's hand and arm clear up to her shoulder. The two scales were sticking up sideways near her wrist like cymbals she was learning to play.

Then Themis started dancing on her pedestal, jiggling side-to-side, and suddenly Major Farnclay stepped from behind her. Judging from his red face and the way he was breathing through his mouth, he'd probably been trying for quite a while to get her chains straightened out while she teetered around like a fidgety kid, making his job twice as hard.

I ran over and started helping.

"Do you suppose we'll ever make a dent on this?" Major Farnclay asked after a while, taking his plaid hat off and wiping his forehead with it.

"We just have to!" was all I could think of to say back.

Finally, we both tugged on the exact right place at the exact right time and the chains loosened themselves and started to come untangled. Almost before we could get our fingers out of the way, the scales tumbled free and hung like they were supposed to, clashing lightly against each other.

"All righty, then!" Major Farnclay said happily, saluting Themis. Then he turned and saluted me. "You must be Miss Capperson. Mrs. Peck has told me many nice things about you."

He stuck out his hand, and after a couple of seconds, I figured out I was supposed to shake it, so I did. "Where *is* she?" I asked. I heard fear in my voice, and that made me realize I *did* feel afraid.

Major Farnclay tented his two index fingers and pressed them against his mouth. Finally he said, "Destiny, Mrs. Peck has had one of her little spells. She's resting in bed this afternoon and her doctor's going to stop by and check her again later, but we're reasonably sure she'll be just fine."

"Her little spells? But . . . I'm her *reader*," I said. "Didn't she ever *tell* you that?"

My chin was out of control, wobbling.

"Yes, yes, she did. Of course she did."

"What *are* her spells? Spells like magical spells? I mean, I *know* they're not like magical spells, but what *are* they?"

Major Farnclay put his hands behind his back and looked up at the sky.

"Mrs. Peck has a bad heart, Destiny. She has what's called congestive heart failure. Sometimes she's fine, but gradually her heart is just . . . giving out on her. Today is a particularly bad day. When you come back next time, she may be much better."

"But . . . but . . . I'm her *reader*," I told him again. This time, I forgot about not letting my chin wobble, and I even had to stop to wipe my nose on my cuff. "You don't understand. She may need me. I won't be any trouble. I won't even talk loud."

"Oh, my dear Miss Capperson, please check back later in the week and . . ."

"Just *please* ask her if she wants me, Major Farnclay! I'll go away if she doesn't! She may just be lying there thinking I didn't come!"

23 • The Darkness around the Edges of Things

You have no idea how glad I am you're here today, Miss Capperson. I was so very afraid things between us would be left forever as tangled as they stood last night."

I knew then that I was so very afraid of things staying like that, too. But how could anything change?

Her bedroom was rose-leaf green. One of her walls had windows from the floor almost to the ceiling so she could see clear across her backyard to the hills that reminded her of Rome and that she'd told me were her favorite view. Her bed was big and had carved wooden posts.

Lying there in that huge bed she seemed too small and fragile to be Mrs. Peck, unless you looked at the deep gardening calluses on her thick, knobby fingers.

Her voice was the same, but not the same. Just as

strong, but in a weak way. Like a recording of a strong, no-nonsense voice turned down very, very low.

I had to remember that she wasn't just Mrs. Peck now, she was also the bad lady, so I tried to sound a little cold as I said, "Do you want me to read something to you?"

"Of course not," she said. It was weird that she was lying so quietly, and only her mouth was moving. "I want to know more about the young boy who was injured in the . . . the accident I was in four years ago. Is he a friend?"

I watched one glistening tear go slowly down her papery cheek.

"Not exactly," I pushed out. "He's got a different last name than mine, but he's my brother. His legs *were* crunched but he had some operations, and most of the time he walks pretty good now."

She closed her eyes when I said that and made a fluttery sound in her throat. Without opening her eyes, she reached over and took my hand.

"Destiny, I want to try and tell you exactly what happened that awful day," she whispered. "I'll have to make this story brief, and I expect that you will pay your usual close attention and draw your usual perceptive conclusions."

She breathed in and out a few times, deep breaths with her mouth open like she was getting ready to take a dive into a deep lake. Then she started talking quietly and fast.

"I was driving my Oldsmobile home from the bank that afternoon, you see, taking a shortcut along an isolated road. Ahead of me, I noticed a driver stopped at an intersecting farm road. He seemed to be staring at me as I approached, watching me in a rather odd way. Just as I neared the intersection, he stepped on his gas and rammed me with his car. He drove his right fender deep into my hood. I was thrown forward and broke my left wrist, a discovery I made when I attempted to open my door to go to his aid.

"Meanwhile, he had backed his car to his previous position and was busily kicking the gravel in the road around rather thoroughly, obscuring our tire tracks. When I managed to struggle from the passenger side of my car, he yelled over to me, 'I'm going to find a phone to call the police. You'll owe big bucks for this, you idiot, because you might have killed my son just now.'"

I gasped and Mrs. Peck turned her head a little bit and looked over at me. She looked awful, like something inside was really hurting her. And when she started talking again her voice was scratchy and even weaker than before.

"You see, Destiny, your brother was too small to be seen over the dashboard. I rushed over to try to help extract him, but I could not because the right fender had pushed inward and his legs were trapped. All I could do was stay there near him until the ambulance arrived."

I braced my elbows on my knees and put my face in my hands.

"I'm sorry for the explicit nature of this story, Destiny, but it *was* a horrible affair. My doctor says the beginning of my macular degeneration that same year was probably connected with my blood pressure being quite high for some months after the . . . accident. The other driver's story to the police was that I sped around the corner, hitting *his* car before pulling back to my own lane and obscuring the tire track evidence. It seems that when an accident is not witnessed and two drivers tell opposite stories, the law these days is reluctant to investigate much further. My insurance adjuster explained to me that there just isn't time or money for that with insurance fraud so common, so generally the two insurance companies simply split the cost. I was not allowed by my insurance company's lawyers or my own to have direct contact with the other driver or even to visit the child, since the other driver had already demanded substantial reimbursement and they were afraid he would find something in my visit to use as provocation for further claims. In return for my promise not to meddle myself, my lawyer has agreed to keep track of the boy . . . I'm sorry, I should say of your brother. I've established a small bank fund that will go to him after my death, or in the event that he needs further treatment before then."

"But you said an avenging Fury made your eyes so you can't read, Mrs. Peck. I looked up avenging Furies in your beautiful book. They only go after *guilty* people, so you *must* think it was your fault, at least partly!"

"That's the true torture of the situation, Destiny," she murmured. "I was not acquitted, so I *feel* convicted. A person like me, who has put such faith in the law, feels guilty when not judged innocent. Did my intellect falter when I saw that man looking at me in an odd way? Was I too slow in my reaction time when the other car came toward me? I wonder, Destiny, can you . . . understand how awful it is to think that I, a teacher, could possibly have caused an innocent child such pain?"

I thought for a long time. "Some girls accused me of cussing, and for a second I thought of myself as a cusser, and then I just suddenly *did* cuss, or at least I said 'idjit,' which I tell my sister is cussing and is really almost worse because it will hurt somebody's feelings. I just did it that once, but I still *feel* like a cusser now."

Mrs. Peck squinted up at the ceiling for a while.

"Yes," she finally said. "I believe my feelings may indeed be somewhat like that."

It was getting a little dark around the edges of things outside. Shadows were moving up the lawn. Mrs. Peck closed her eyes again.

"Mrs. Peck?" I whispered after a while.

She squeezed my hand to tell me to go on.

"Remember the second day I worked for you, when you told me about the Oracle of Delphi answering everybody's tough questions? Do we have anything like that now? It would be so great if there was somebody who knew all the answers, and you could just go up to them and ask them."

Mrs. Peck made a strange sound, sort of a gurgle. At first I thought she was choking, but I leaned closer to her face and saw she was chuckling.

"The Oracle of Delphi didn't know beans, Destiny. She was simply able to give answers that were open to interpretation. A famous ruler, for instance, wanted to attack another ruler, and asked the Oracle if he should. The Oracle answered, 'If you do, a great kingdom will fall.' The ruler took this to mean he would be successful, so he attacked and was roundly defeated. The fallen kingdom, you see, was his own."

I nodded slowly, thinking about that.

"Still," she continued, "the way people interpreted what the Oracle said could surely have told them a lot about themselves, if they'd stopped to think."

She'd lost me.

"All I want to know is this, Mrs. Peck. Just this. Who *can* you believe when everybody's telling you different stuff about life?"

She didn't open her eyes, but she smiled and squeezed my hand harder and answered in a strong voice almost like her usual one.

"Yourself, Destiny Louise Capperson," she said. "Believe in *you*."

24 • TREASURE

My mother was standing in the kitchen with Helena when I got home that afternoon. Helena was wearing a long orange dress with rhinestones along the neck and she had lots of gold chains woven into her purplish-black hair. She was puffing on a cigarette in a gold plastic cigarette holder. Mama had on the almost-leather yellow jumpsuit she got with the fifty-dollar winning ticket Jack scratched that time. On the floor between them was a shiny purple suitcase with the name HELENA spelled out in gold stars on it, some plastic Wal-Mart bags full of clothes, and Ethelene. Ethelene held her arms up to me and bounced on her fat bottom, so I picked her up and balanced her on my hip.

"Do you think you could please give me back the two-hundred-dollar lottery ticket?" I asked Mama.

She looked at Helena, then back at me. "No way!"

she said, laughing and bending to scoop the handles of the three Wal-Mart bags over her arm. "Helena and Ethelene and me are on our way to California right here as we speak! Helena's got that winner ticket all safe in her shoulder bag, and we'll cash it in on our way to the bus station. All's we been waiting for is you to get home and take care of Bert. And where's Nathan gallivanted off to, anyhow?"

"Shup?" Ethelene said softly, pushing her face into my neck.

Mama held her open arm out for me to pass her Ethelene, but I took a step backwards, shaking my head. "What about Jack?" I asked. My voice sounded squeaky, so I cleared my throat. "Is he in jail or out? Did you decide to lie and tell the police he was here last weekend, when he was probably out burning down that restaurant?"

I was shocked at the words coming out of my mouth, and even more shocked that she didn't yell at me about them.

"Destiny, when I get back from Hollywood with that jackpot money, I'll deal with all that," she said in a voice like you'd use to talk to someone Ethelene's age. "For right now, I have just *got* to get away from all this and have a good time with no worries for a while. Is that so very much to ask?"

"I think you think Jack did it," I said quickly, before I could make myself stop. "And if they let him out of jail while you're gone he might do something else real bad, maybe even to one of us, your kids. He forces people to sell rotten potatoes, after all. *And he sells other people's perfectly good pets.*"

Those sounded like pretty lame reasons to be afraid of someone, even to me. But I *was* afraid. What was *really* worrying me about Jack coming home while she was gone?

Mama looked at the ceiling and put her hand on her hip like she was gathering every bit of patience she could.

"All right, Destiny. Maybe I do have some little bit of an idea that Jack *might* have helped burn down that restaurant. But nobody got hurt but some big dumb insurance company that deserved it! How can you think Jack would *hurt* anybody?"

When she asked that question, it just sort of opened a window in my brain and, almost oracle-like, I *knew* the answer. I just hoped when I told it to *her* she wouldn't go ballistic and ground me forever for being vicious and smart-mouthed.

"Mama, Nathan was too little to see over the dashboard the afternoon of the accident four years ago, but he just started remembering something he heard. He says Jack selling his rabbits jolted his memory. Nathan remembers now that right one second before the wreck Jack said to him, 'You keep still and this will be our last afternoon before good times.' Mama? Think . . . think about what Jack could have meant by that."

My mother just stood there staring at me, looking bewildered and shaking her head.

But Helena got it, all right. Her mouth fell open and the cigarette holder hit the floor. She toed out the flame on our linoleum. "That just cuts it, Virginia. Don't you call me no more, you hear? Burning down a restaurant for insurance is bad enough, but endangering the life of a kid for it? That boyfriend of yours is a dangerous criminal, girl!"

Mama dropped her right arm and the three Wal-Mart sacks came sliding off—plop, plop, plop. "Dangerous . . . criminal?" she whispered. "But Jack told me he was minding his own business that afternoon, driving real slow, and this hysterical old lady . . ."

Helena threw up her arms. "Virginia? Hel-lo! Earth calling! Has it never occurred to you that Jack *lies* like a rug? Don't you know that, really?"

"How do I know what I know?" Mama moaned, pulling at her hair. "I just always feel so . . . so *overwhelmed!*"

Helena snatched up her suitcase and stomped toward the door. "Well, get over it, Virginia! You don't need a professional psychic. You just need to grow up!"

A couple of seconds after the front door slammed behind Helena, we heard the dogs around the alley trash cans howling. Then a few seconds after that, we heard Nate's sneakers pounding unevenly up the back stairs and the back door banged open.

"Baby!" Mama sobbed, dropping to her knees and holding out her arms to him. "Nathan, baby!"

I put Ethelene down and ran over to switch on the overhead light. Nathan was filthy, and his jacket was soaked with sweat around the neck.

"I gotta *show* you, Mom!" He ran over to her. "I *finally* found your *treasure!*"

He unsnapped his jacket with one hard yank. Snug and protected beneath his left arm was a muddy piece of cardboard he must have found on the ground near one of the Dumpsters out at The Penitentiary—orange cardboard, possibly part of a Wheaties box.

He began unfolding it while our mother watched with her hands over her mouth and with black mascara running like twin rivers down her cheeks.

"There it is. Your ruby ring you gave me to keep safe for you!" Nathan announced in a breathless voice, bouncing on his heels as he proudly held the ring out to her.

It was one of those gold plastic rings you get in quarter machines—the kind where you can push in the two sides to adjust the size. It had a huge red plastic stone.

My mother told me later it had been the free prize in a box of cereal she'd opened the morning of the accident.

Still, I'd say she thought of it now as priceless treasure. Also, it must have made her know what she knew. Because she slipped it on her little finger as carefully as you would a real ruby, then she grabbed Nate and started kissing his sweaty face and neck over and over again, evidently not even caring that he smelled like wet garbage.

25 • Born of the Just Heavens

Suddenly I just wanted to lie down right there on the kitchen linoleum and sleep for about a million years. Too exhausted even to walk, I crawled up the stairs, hoping Ethelene wouldn't see me doing it, and went on to bed.

I slept like a potato and woke up real early the next morning. I lay there wondering if Nathan had taken my carving knife or my scissors out to The Penitentiary to dig with yesterday. I finally decided I'd better run out there before school to look and see if he'd left anything behind.

I was probably halfway to the trailer court before I admitted to myself that I was really going out there to ask Nathan's smelly oracle a hard question or two.

The Penitentiary seemed almost magical that morning. The smoke that wafted through it from the burning tires down the road was pinkish and sparkling with cinders and dawn light. The chain-link fence was dripping with silver dew and the top of each light post dissolved into the mist like Jack's beanpole disappearing into a cloud.

The bony trees that guarded Dead Man's Swamp looked like skeleton hands clutching at the fog. I crept as close to the oracle as I could stand to. I cleared my throat and stood holding my nose and breathing through my mouth.

"Oh Oracle of Dead Man's Swamp," I began, "play along with something for a second, okay? Let's pretend we're looking at Themis's scales, and a tiny little Mrs. Peck is in one and a tiny little Jack is in the other one. Mrs. Peck believes the law is everything. Jack, on the other hand, believes in getting by with anything he can. So the scales go way down on his side—he's busted. Still, it gets nerve-wracking having your electricity and phone shut off and not taking your kids to the doctor when you need to. So don't you think Mrs. Peck's side of the scale might go down a tiny bit, too, just because of her getting to be so automatically rich and lucky when other people automatically aren't? I mean, I know Helena is going to keep the lottery ticket for back pay that Mama owes her, but was it really so bad for me to take it from Mrs. Peck? Because wasn't that really like just trying to even the scales a tiny little bit without really hurting anyone?"

"You are right, my child," the oracle said in a squeaky version of my own voice.

But I shouldn't have added that last phrase, the one about not hurting anyone. It reminded me of Jack probably not meaning to hurt anyone, either, but doing it big-time anyhow.

"Yes, you are *right,* my child!" the oracle repeated.

But it wasn't enough, because I felt my hand going into my jacket pocket, like I was hoping against hope I'd somehow still find that lottery ticket there.

•　•　•

Miss Valentino showed one of the videos from the library in Art I that day. It wasn't even really about art. It was about the rain forest, which is colorful, of course, but not really art. Miss Valentino didn't try to tie it in, either. She just sat watching along with us, and when the bell rang, she hurried out into the hall before everyone was out of the room. Well, actually, before everyone but me was out of the room.

I followed her as she walked quickly down the hall. I was pretty sure she knew I was back there, but she didn't turn around. It was almost like she thought I was one of those Furies, chasing her. Finally I had to say, "Uh, Miss Valentino?"

She stopped and just stood still with her shoulders sort of stiff. Finally, she turned to me. "Oh! Hi, Dess!" she said, as though I hadn't just been in her class.

"Hi," I said. "Uh, I'm sorry to bother you, but I just thought you might want to know that Mrs. Peck was sick yesterday. I'm going out there right now to check on her."

Now she looked worried and interested. "Sick?" she said.

"She has this heart thing, but she's supposed to be okay again, maybe even today. But, well, I just wanted to ask you real quick. Remember when you told me about the play in her class, and her flunking you and some other kids that went to the soccer game? Well, what I wanted to know is, what do you think she would have done if one of you had actually, uh, *stolen* something from her, or something like that?"

Miss Valentino frowned. "Dess, do you think she *needs* anything? Is there anything you can think of I could do for her?"

I shook my head—not a "no" shake, an "I don't get it" shake. "Why do you care so much about her?" I asked, trying to get the subject back to my question. I was actually feeling a little mad at Miss Valentino about the *Rain Forest* video, but I knew that was dumb. "She must have been your worst teacher ever, being so hard like that."

"She was my best," Miss Valentino said. "*Because* she was so hard. I don't expect you to know what I'm talking about at your age, Dess. When you're older and thinking back to *how* you learned *what* you learned, you may understand."

My throat filled up with something hot. "When

you're older and being a not-teacher in dumb old France you may understand what I'm feeling, too!" I blurted. I turned and ran away from her then, out to bus 4.

•   •   •

In a way, I was almost glad I was so miserable about yelling at Miss Valentino because it gave my brain less room to dread confessing to Mrs. Peck. There was no good or easy way to do it. I decided on the bus that if Mrs. Peck felt good enough to listen, I'd just tell her. No excuses, no leading up to it, no nothing. Just out with it.

When I got off the bus and started up her lane, things seemed normal. But partway up, I began to get the creeps. The beautiful lane seemed sucked dry of its noise and energy. It was like the leaves of the tree canopy had turned into fakes, just dusty plastic, and the breeze I'd thought was so magical had only been coming from a hidden electric fan that had finally shorted out and stopped.

I could barely find enough oxygen to breathe.

I panicked and started running up the hill. I was dizzy from gulping down all that still air when I finally plunged out of the leaf canopy, and at first I was really relieved to be in the open garden. But then the garden felt strange to me, too. The roses weren't bobbing, and the birds and butterflies were keeping their distance. The clouds just hung motionless up there in the sky like white ships tied to a bright blue dock.

"Mrs. Peck?" I whisper-called. I cleared my throat and called louder. "Mrs. Peck!"

At the sound of my voice, a huge wedge of brown birds rose from one of the rigid poplar trees near me and flew away without chirping. I turned, startled, to watch them, and finally saw Mrs. Peck sitting on the garden swing. She was smaller. She was whiter and very still. She was propped against some pillows with her hands in her lap.

I ran to her. I didn't dare flop down into the swing beside her. I had the strange fear that just moving it would break her feet off at the ankles.

"Miss Capperson," she said, lifting one hand slowly, slowly from her lap and putting it down beside her on the swing. "I'm delighted. Come, sit."

I eased down to the swing as gently as I could. "Thanks," I whispered.

She turned her head and looked at me directly by staring at my shoulder.

"I stole your lottery ticket, Mrs. Peck!" I blurted. "It was worth two hundred dollars and I stole it and I can't get it to give it back! I was thinking I could work for you for free fifty times, or more if you want. I'll do whatever you say about it!"

I covered my face with my hands, too ashamed to look at her. I could tell she was still looking at *me,* though. Just looking, without saying a word. After a while I peeked out from between my fingers, then lowered my hands to my lap and dropped my head.

She began moving the swing with her feet, just the tiniest little movement, forward and back. Why didn't she just start yelling at me and get it over with? Or maybe she was working up to saying she was disappointed in me, which would be even worse.

"Destiny, I've been wondering if you've gotten around to reading the section of the mythology book that concerns your name."

I shook my head. The guilt I was feeling was worse than the guilt about selling rotten potatoes, worse even than the guilt about not keeping my rabbit-protecting promise to Nathan. I hadn't had much control over those things, but this thing I had. I *had!*

"The Destinies were three goddesses, you see— Clotho, Lachesis, and Atropos. Between them, they controlled all mortal lives. Clotho spun the thread of life, Lachesis held it up and figured out how long to make it, and Atropos cut it off. Their father was none other than the great Zeus, god of the heavens."

Mrs. Peck stopped her story and stopped her feet. "Miss Capperson, it's just occurred to me that this isn't your usual workday. Did you come all the way out here simply to report that you'd stolen something belonging to me?"

I shook my head, still too ashamed to meet her eyes. "I came to see how you were feeling," I pushed out.

I heard her take a deep breath. "My vigor appears to be on the wane. Atropos will soon be cutting the thread of my life, and that means there's much to be done. I've willed this place to the public library, you see. Major Farnclay has been so kind as to consent to be my executor, which means he'll be in charge of getting things in the house and on the property ready for that transition."

Mrs. Peck reached over and grabbed my wrist. She squeezed it, hard.

"He'll require *help*, Miss Capperson."

I understood that this was how I was supposed to pay for the ticket. Something just sort of came apart inside of me, some big, tight bubble burst. I could breathe right again, and I realized I'd been so afraid she'd tell me just to forget about it. "I'll be here, Mrs. Peck," I said, looking into her eyes.

"Good," she said, and smiled. She put her head back against the pillows. "Good, that's very good. He's coming later. I'll tell him. He'll be delighted."

I felt her hand go limp, and I lifted it and put it back onto her lap. I thought she was sleeping, so I inched forward, trying to get off the swing without moving it.

"I expected you to display your usual lively curiosity regarding the *mother* of the Destinies," she suddenly said quietly, not opening her eyes. "The mother of Clotho, Lachesis, and Atropos was none other than your favorite—Themis, the blindfolded birdbath girl in our rose garden. Fathered by Zeus, mothered by Justice, the Destinies, you see, were born from the just heavens. It's a fine classical concept, which you yourself do not dishonor, Miss Capperson."

I sagged back into the swing and stared at the sky. *Destiny Louise Capperson, born from the just heavens.* The idea took my breath away.

"Mrs. Peck?" I whispered after a while. "Are . . . are you too tired to give me your definition of hope? Like Pandora saw down in the bottom of that jar?"

She didn't answer for a while. Then she whispered, "Give me back your hand, will you, Destiny?"

I slipped my hand under hers again, and she squeezed it.

"I've always believed Pandora probably saw her own reflection," Mrs. Peck told me. "To hope is to look yourself in the eye and realize you're capable of doing and being anything you really want to in this imperfect but fascinating world."

26 • MAMA ACTS GOOFY

When I got home that afternoon, everybody was in the driveway and there was an extra car beside Jack's truck. Its hood was up, and Mama was bent way down into it with Ethelene sitting on her left foot. Nathan was over in the grass a little bit to the side. He was holding Bert around the waist and swimming her through the air, and Bert was flapping her arms around and laughing her head off.

When I got close enough to pick up Ethelene, I saw Rachel's mother behind the wheel of the car. She was frowning, and a little tip of her tongue was showing between her clenched lips.

Mama pulled her arms from the car's insides and yelled over to Mrs. Nichols, "Hit it again!" Mrs. Nichols leaned forward and turned the key, and there was a little flash under the hood. "It sparks when I shortwire the terminals, so there's juice in the battery!" Mama yelled to Mrs. Nichols. "Hit your headlights!" They went on and off. "Battery's up enough, so there should be charge to turn it over! I'm worried it's the starter!"

Mama ducked into the car's guts again, then a couple of minutes later stood up and slammed the hood down. She walked over to Mrs. Nichols's window. "I better just run you on home," she said, "and tomorrow I could see about getting some new brushes to put in that starter for you."

•   •   •

When she got back from taking Mrs. Nichols home, Mama acted all goofy, dancing around the kitchen while we got dinner and cleaned up, then singing silly little songs and throwing wet washcloths at people while we gave the girls their baths. Her goofiness made us all feel good. Except for the night when she bought the tickets and called herself Hurricane Virginia, she hadn't let go like that for quite a while.

After the little kids were in bed, the two of us flopped onto the sofa. We slumped in the saggy middle spot, leaning together.

"Mama?" I asked quietly. "What would be your definition of hope?"

She lifted her pinky finger and the ring Nathan had given her caught the light and looked even more scratched up than it usually did. Her long, fancy purple nails looked pretty scratched up, too, and they had grease around the edges.

"Hope? I tell you what, Destiny, my brain is tired tonight. All I can think of is this character on one of my soap operas named Hope. Can I get back to you?"

"Sure," I said, snuggling closer.

She put her cheek against my hair. "Dess, this morning I told the police Jack was gone all last weekend," she said softly. "I signed a sworn statement, in fact. I got the distinct impression he'll be out of commission for a while now, and he'd better not even *try* to ever come back here, either."

My art notebook was right there on the coffee table. I decided to show her "Bus Barrettes." She loved it so much that I tore it out for her and put it on her lap.

"Destiny, you're a person of unusual talents and skills, you know that?"

"I could make you a frame for it from duct tape if you want," I told her. I was flustered. I couldn't remember her ever complimenting me like that before.

"That'd be nice."

We just sat quietly like that for a while, looking at the picture.

"What was the deal with Mrs. Nichols?" I asked.

"She came over here to talk to me about that class of hers, and then when she went to leave, her car wouldn't start. She gave me money to get the parts, and tomorrow I'll put new brushes in the starter for her."

Mama put my picture on the sofa beside her and leaned forward with her elbows on her knees. She covered her face with her hands and said, "Dess, when I was driving Nancy Nichols home this evening, she told me the strangest thing. She told me it wasn't normal for someone to know their way around the insides of a vehicle like I do. She said people are crying out for good mechanics, and I could get, something . . . certified? I could get certified to do that kind of work by going to the junior college at the same time I'm getting my GED, and then I could make real good money. Can you imagine? All my life I've kept vehicles running, first my daddy's and then when he left, whoever else's was around, and no one has ever said a thing about paying me or me being good at it. Or good at anything, for that matter."

Suddenly, she was sobbing there with her hands over her face.

"Well, I've always thought you were a person of unusual talents and skills," I told her, hoping to make her laugh, which she did. Laughed and cried at once.

• • •

I owed Miss Valentino an apology for smart-mouthing. I decided to carve a potato zebra for her that night, and I worked hard to make it my best one ever.

I took it to school the next morning, but I decided against leaving it inside my hot locker. I was arranging it on the corner of my homeroom desk right before school when Samantha and Rachel and Crystal came into the room together. Rachel and Samantha went right to their desks, but Crystal had her wand in her hand and she stopped by my desk and bounced it around on my zebra's back.

"Come to life, little lifeless animal!" she commanded. "Oh come to life! Come to life!"

"Quit," I said.

"You didn't make that zebra," she said.

"Yes I did," I said.

"You did not, either," she said.

"I did so," I said. "I carved it out of a potato."

Crystal turned and yelled for Rachel and Samantha to come over, and when they were all three beside my desk, Rachel said, "You didn't make that little zebra there."

"Yes she did," Crystal said. "Out of a potato."

Rachel looked at me. "You should include free carving lessons for your customers and their friends with the potatoes you sell."

"I'll show you how to carve if you want, but I'm *not* a potato girl like you called me that day in your yard," I told her firmly. "I'm going to be an artist like Miss Valentino, so you could call me an artist. Or right now I'm Mrs. Peck's reader, so you could also call me that."

"Well, *I'm* just going to call you Destiny," Crystal said, twirling her wand through her fingers like a baton and prancing to her desk.

• • •

I took the potato zebra in to give to Miss Valentino during lunch period.

"You amaze me, as usual," Miss Valentino said with
a deep sigh. She was pulling apart an orange, and she offered me half. "What did you use for the eyelashes?"

"The little tips of some of those toothpicks I painted
for your Eiffel Tower."

This was the first time I'd done eyelashes, not just on
a zebra but on any animal. I had to admit they looked
pretty wonderful.

I watched my thumb push seeds from an orange slice
as I said, "Miss Valentino? I'm really sorry about the way
I talked to you after Art One yesterday. I'm especially
sorry I called France dumb."

She smiled and shrugged. She seemed sad. "How
was Mrs. Peck yesterday, Dess?"

An idea came exploding out of my mouth, along with
a little orange juice.

"You could come with me to work this afternoon and
see her yourself!"

Miss Valentino looked surprised, then puzzled. Then
she said, "Okay, it's a date. Meet me at the Valiant right
after school."

27 • MYSTERY AND BEAUTY

Miss Valentino draped this long orange scarf over her hair to keep it from whipping around too much in the breeze from the open car windows.

"I'm glad we'll have this chance to talk, Destiny," she said as we pulled from the school parking lot. "I've been worried you're thinking awful things about me. For . . . for quitting. I mean, for . . . moving to France."

"The kids in Art One are rude and childish," I said. "That's my opinion. It serves them right to lose you as a wonderful teacher."

"Wonderful teacher," she said, then laughed in a sad way and whispered, "right."

"You have wonderful things to teach and they don't listen. I don't even blame you for giving up and showing the *Rain Forest* video. They should just *try!*"

I glanced over at her and saw that the tip of her nose was red and her knuckles on the steering wheel were white. "I just . . . just wanted to make a difference! I just wanted to show them that art is an exciting way of looking at the world, was that too much to ask?"

I shook my head sadly. "*I* sure never thought it was."

We rode without talking for a couple of blocks, then she said, "I know Mrs. Peck will be disappointed in me. Remember when she said I was an 'educator'?"

I nodded, trying hard to think of something to cheer her up.

"Here's how I picture it," I said. "Okay, let's pretend it's ten years from now and Max and Russell are offered these jobs drawing comic book superheroes. And their boss says, 'Of course, you know you have to put perspective in these drawings so it looks like the vicious villains are flying through the air and stuff, don't you?' and Russell says to himself, 'Ohmigosh! Perspective! That's that thing Miss Valentino tried to teach us!' And Max whispers to Russell, 'Maybe we can remember enough about that to try and do it before we lose our jobs!' And so they work really hard and learn to do it, remembering your instructions and knowing all the time how much easier their lives would be now if they'd just practiced back in Art One like they were supposed to."

Miss Valentino laughed. "Oh, Dess, you're a hoot," she said.

That kind of hurt my feelings. I'd been trying to make a serious point.

"You don't think it'll happen. But I'll bet that's what *you* thought when Mrs. Peck gave you that F for missing the play back in eighth grade. I bet at the time you thought, 'She's just mean, so who cares?' But now you say she was your best teacher and you learned all kinds of junk you didn't know you were learning. People don't always know what's getting crammed into their heads, that's all I'm saying."

We'd reached the turn into Mrs. Peck's lane. Like that first day, Miss Valentino had trouble finding the opening in the bushes, only this time I could point it out to her.

"Watch out for a man on a bicycle," I added.

The sun coming through what was left of the leaf canopy painted moving light-stripes across our windshield, and across Miss Valentino when I looked over at her.

"You said I'd be a not-teacher," she whispered, so softly I barely heard. "That really, really hurt, to think of myself that way."

I wished I could take that back, if it had hurt her like that. But it was the simple truth.

"Oh! I meant to tell you something!" I said, swiveling in my seat to face her, pulling my ankle up under my leg. "You know Jacqui? Well, I saw her out on the playground actually *drawing* a necklace and a crown on one of her

unicorns. *Drawing* it, not tracing. I mean, she might have
gone on just tracing forever if you hadn't . . ."

I stopped in the middle of that sentence because I'd
just noticed something. "Miss Valentino! You got rid of
that rabbit's foot!"

A little oval mirror with rhinestones hung from her
keyring instead.

She shrugged and smiled. "I saw your point, Dess. In
fact, that very night, when I was checking out the consignment auction and buying all that art stuff I showed
you? Well, this guy had just bought these rabbits when I
got there, and he was talking about how good they were
going to taste, so I offered him ten dollars more than he'd
paid for them. I just kept thinking of what you'd said to
me that afternoon, about how a rabbit could have once
been someone's pet. I'm trying to find a different home
for them, though. I can't even go out of town for one
weekend with those rabbits to take care of."

To tell you the truth, adrenaline or something was
sizzling happily through my veins by then and I couldn't
pay as close attention to Miss Valentino's problems as I
had before.

"She's bound to call me an educator," I heard her re-
peat in a very small voice. We were at the top of the lane,
under the big cottonwood tree, and then we rolled over
the last little hump of ground and could suddenly see
the whole front garden and the house.

Mrs. Peck was sitting on the garden swing. She was

small, and white as one of her statues. She had a book in her lap. I'd soon be reading to her from that book.

"*Look* at her, Dess," Miss Valentino whispered.

Mrs. Peck had seen our car and now she was standing up. She tented her hands over her eyes to shield them from the sun and squared her shoulders, watching us.

"*Look* at her," Miss Valentino repeated. "*Feel* her! She's such a . . ."

"*Tea*cher," I said.

"I *could* go to France for Christmas, then come back and finish the year," Miss Valentino said, still looking at Mrs. Peck. "Give it my best shot, I mean."

Mrs. Peck stood perfectly still, waiting for us. It was almost like with her steady gaze she was pulling us over the top of the hill and out into the bright sunshine.

•   •   •

I got to tell Nathan about his rabbits coming home before Miss Valentino brought them over to us today. I decided to build up to it slowly so I could anticipate his surprise, anticipation being a favorite thing of Mrs. Peck's and mine both.

We were hanging out on our back step. Nathan was coloring the toe of his cowboy boot with a purple crayon.

"So, Nathan," I said casually, "have you thought any more about hiring that detective you were talking about to look for your rabbits?"

He glanced up at me through his bangs, then switched to the other toe. "Mom doesn't want to sell the ring and get the million dollars," he murmured. "She said she doesn't want to take it off for a single minute, even. I gotta save up money some other way. I'm thinking about fixing boots for people. Making them more fancy."

I nodded. "Coloring them, you mean?"

He nodded. "And I could sell bologna sandwiches on the side."

I just couldn't sit still any longer. I needed to laugh and giggle and jump up and down, but then Nathan would ask me what was going on and I'd have to tell him and give up my anticipation. So I stood and walked over to the old refrigerator. "Come and help me fix up the rabbit apartment building," I called over my shoulder.

By the time I got my roll of duct tape off my wrist, Nathan was by my side, waiting for instructions. "We need to refasten the screen wire. I'll measure and you tape," I told him. "Remember to leave one corner a little loose."

"So we can give them food," Nathan said. "You promise someday they'll be eating here again, Destiny?" He sighed. "I forgot. I'm not supposed to say 'promise.'"

I heard Miss Valentino's car pull into the driveway. I felt happy, but also like I was suddenly about to cry. "This time you can say promise," I said softly to my brother.

• • •

It's pretty late now, but the sky is clear and the moon is bright enough to draw by. Nathan is in his sleeping bag on the floor of our room, along with the rabbits, who are in the great cage Miss Valentino bought and decorated for them. The cage has these little fake vines twining through the wire on the sides, and it's painted orange and green and purple. Mama said Nathan could have the rabbits in the living room with him tonight, right beside the couch. But he wanted to be on the floor with them, and Ethelene wanted him to bring them up here. It's cozy, all of us, kids and rabbits, together like this.

Snowball isn't in the cage—she's sleeping on Nathan's pillow, curved around the top of his head like a big white wig. I thought about trying to carve her, but the potatoes are getting too soft to carve. And besides, it's not just Snowball I want to keep tonight, like you keep things with art.

It's the way Nathan made this little sound, sort of a gasp, then stood straining forward there by the old refrigerator this afternoon right after Mama and Miss Valentino appeared around the corner of the house, clumsily dragging the rabbit cage behind them. It's the way he finally trusted his hopes and ran like a blur through the yard. It's the way he buried his face in Snowball's soft fur, and the way she kept happily sniffing his neck as he carried her around all evening. It's the way

Mama couldn't take her eyes off him and smiled so wide and the way the flickery overhead light in the kitchen sent sparks off her ruby ring, and it's the way the little girls kept patting the rabbits on their ears and kissing them and getting fur in their mouths and spitting and giggling. It's Miss Valentino in her Valiant and Mrs. Peck in her garden of roses and statues.

Can anybody, even one of those famous French painters, capture real life and make it stay forever like it truly is? That's what I'd like to know.

I guess you just have to buckle down and try. *Destiny Louise Capperson, born of the just heavens.* With the moon so bright and the stars so close, even the broken televisions out by the onion patch look mysterious and beautiful tonight.